An Imperfect Man

An Imperfect Man

John Calabro

QUATTRO BOOKS

The publication of *An Imperfect Man* has been generously supported by the Canada Council for the Arts and the Ontario Arts Council.

Cover design: Sarah Beaudin
Cover sculpture: Julie Campagna (www.campagnabronze.com)
Typography: Natasha Shaikh
Editors: Allan Briesmaster and Luciano Iacobelli

Library and Archives Canada Cataloguing in Publication

Calabro, John, author
        An imperfect man / John Calabro.

ISBN 978-1-926802-80-0 (paperback)

        I. Title.

PS8605.A43I46 2015   C813'.6   C2014-905815-2

Published by Quattro Books Inc.
Toronto, Ontario
www.quattrobooks.ca

Printed in Canada

To Louis, Claudia, Aliza and Shannon

And

To all misunderstood parents and their
misunderstood children

"The mistake one makes is to speak to people."
—Samuel Beckett

"I scath a chéile a mhaireann na daoine."
"People live in each other's shadows."
—Irish proverb

1.

I open the front door and finally, a warm, sunny day, a day of bright yellow sunshine with a lazy blue sky over the canopy of budding trees, a day where the smell of fresh grass and young flowers popping up amid the English gardens peppering Wilson Park Road might tempt one to call this morning a perfect morning. I take a deep, deep breath and slowly, very slowly, deliberately, between pressed lips, release it.

And then it spoils.

A woman's voice.

Directed at me.

I am already on the sidewalk, eyeing Queen Street up ahead, on my way to work, and I should simply keep walking, ignore this discordant chirp, but it is instinctive, stronger than me. Turning my head slightly, I see her coming out from between the two houses, pushing an unruly garbage bin. Our eyes meet and she now knows that I've seen her. Our houses are the only ones with a flat, clear path to the sidewalk; the others on this small Toronto street in Parkdale are perched on a slant or hidden behind massive trees. This sleepy, hillside stretch of street between King and Queen, and steps from the lake, is where I have lived my whole life.

"Hello, neighbour," she repeats louder, and in a way-too-perky voice for this time of the morning.

I fully turn around and face her.

It is my neighbour who lives next door, at Number 48, and who I don't really know. She is mostly a stranger to me; the proximity of our houses is the only excuse for our connection, but then, all the houses are close to each other in this neighbourhood. The tree branches on each side of the street, when in full foliage, arch towards each other and meet high above the road to make the whole area cozy and slightly claustrophobic. I don't know the name of this neighbour, and I am fine with that anonymity. It's not that I don't like people; I am shy by nature and don't do well in social situations. I either don't say very much, bordering on autism, or babble on too long, bordering on manic. I know most of the people on this street, and her, by sight, but like with all my other neighbours, I have done the polite salutation *thing*—a word or two, a quick wave of the hand, but nothing more. My trick to avoidance is to keep on walking, while disgorging a few courteous words, which allows me to sidestep the awkwardness of a prolonged conversation. I am not comfortable talking to people for the sake of just talking, never was. Unfortunately, by stopping and turning around instead of continuing to walk, I am now committed.

"Good morning," I say politely, "nice day."

Conversation over, I quickly turn away from her.

"What happened to your arm?" she yells, and I stop.

I had momentarily forgotten about the arm strapped against my chest. I now feel even worse for not having completely ignored her in the first place, and for having added the "nice day" to my short greeting, for having implied that I was friendly, or inclined to talk, for having misrepresented myself. In my defence it was a beautiful day.

"Nothing, I fell down the stairs... and... sprained it," I yell back.

"What?"

A car honks and the subsequent squealing of tires makes it difficult for us to hear each other. Instead of accepting this natural obstruction to conversing and going back to her house, she leaves the bin at the curb and begins walking towards me, ostensibly to better hear me.

I begin to panic, I sort out in my head what one can legitimately sprain in a fall and how it might have happened. Did I sprain a shoulder, an elbow, or a wrist? And which of those would warrant a sling? Suddenly remembering that last year a colleague of mine had said, "I sprained my wrist," I decide on a wrist as a lie. But did he wear a sling? It seems silly to wear one just for a wrist. I don't recall he did and instantly I make another choice.

"I sprained my shoulder," I blurt out.

The traffic noises subside and my voice is louder than it needs to be, and I don't like it. I am not a loud person.

Standing in front of me, I get to see my neighbour up close. It is the first time since she moved in next door. She and a man who I assumed was her husband moved in last fall, and with the arrival of a long Toronto winter, and my tendencies to avoid people, we had not introduced ourselves.

"Does it hurt?" she asks, in an overly sympathetic voice that I am not sure is any better than the earlier perkiness, but it is a warm tone which makes it difficult to ignore. She stares at my arm in its makeshift sling as she says that. Maybe I shouldn't have used my mother's old silk scarf to anchor my arm to my chest.

I stare back and scrutinize this woman.

She looks a bit lost in an oversized grey Roots sweatshirt and skinny black tights. Her light brown hair is pulled back in a severe ponytail that dangles a few inches above her neck. She is not wearing any makeup and looks pale under the bright morning sun. Waif-like, I find her smaller, thinner and older than I had thought, maybe just slightly younger than me.

It was late October when they moved in and I happened to be on the porch smoking a cigarette when the truck arrived. I had a mild curiosity to see who had purchased the house next door, but not enough to go over and talk to them. I stubbed the cigarette out and went inside to watch discreetly from my mother's bedroom. Her window opened onto the porch and gave me a full view of the street.

"No. Just a bit," I answer, in a flat, noncommittal tone. I was not sure what to do next or what to say. I would like to make up for my past discourtesy but don't know how. A wave of anxiety comes over me and I feel my face turning red.

I stay planted, looking at her. Seeing her up close I cannot say that she is beautiful, but I would not call her ugly, I would say average, quite normal, very indistinguishable. Thin, and not very tall, she wears conventional glasses, small square lenses in a black frame that don't do much for her. She also has an unusually round face, which I guess in some ways makes her distinguishable, or at least noticeable. Under normal circumstances I would not gawk for so long, but this morning I uncharacteristically do, as if trying to be a better neighbour, a better person.

She looks at me scrutinizing her. Her face goes quickly from sympathetic, to glum, to concern. I had been staring intensely without saying anything, like an idiot, mostly because I didn't know what to say, I couldn't come up with anything. I was not being rude, but maybe she just realized that I might be a psycho, or at the very least that she had just introduced herself to a strange, unlikeable neighbour.

She puts her head down and mumbles something.

Instead of ending this awkward moment by saying, "Bye," smiling and leaving, I continue to look at her, trying to think of something to say that would not leave a bad impression. Generally, I want people to like me, even though I have issues being around them.

In a warmer, kinder tone, I say, "Sorry… I should have introduced myself before, how rude of me… welcome to the neighbourhood, my name is Jack."

"Hi, my name is Lisa." She is not convinced that I am sincere, and I can hear it in her unsteady voice.

We shake hands. I smile, as genuinely as I can muster.

She regains her composure, returns my smile, "Nice to meet you, Jack."

Behind me, I can hear the rattling of a streetcar and it reminds me that I am going to be late for work.

"You are a teacher, right?"

I am surprised that she knows that, and the look on my face reveals it.

"Elizabeth told me," and she points across the street. "Apparently, she knows everything about everyone."

She winks at me, letting me know that she has also quickly realized that Elizabeth is someone who likes to gossip. Elizabeth, whose English pedigree made her superior, never got along with my mother. She didn't like that we were Irish, that we had lodgers; she looked down on us and eyed our tenants with suspicion.

"Yes… which reminds me, I must get going if I don't want to be late, which I think I already am—at least I've a good excuse."

She brushes away a strand of hair from her forehead. Her head is not that round once you get used to it, and she is not *that* unattractive. I keep looking at her and don't move.

"Sorry for having bothered you, Jack. I'm glad we finally met."

It is my cue to leave.

"Me too… and what do you do, Lisa?"

There is definitely something wrong with me this morning, I don't usually do questions and answers with neighbours. I don't extend conversations, I shorten them, end them if I can.

"I am a nurse at St. Joseph, you know, the hospital just over there."

I know that hospital quite well—west of Roncesvalles, beside the streetcar barns, I would take my mother there when she first got sick. The nurses were all so nice, and I quickly wonder if I might have seen her there, but I can't be sure, those days were a blur.

"That must be quite a challenge, but now I really have to run and catch a streetcar," I say to her.

"OK, have a good day, Jack. Nice talking to you… Hey Jack, do you want me to put your garbage bin out?"

I hadn't bothered, I seldom remembered, often leaving it parked to the side of the house for weeks. Not that it was ever full; since my mother passed away and the tenants left, I didn't shop very much nor did I like cooking for myself.

"OK. Thanks."

I walk up towards the streetcar stop which is not far away from the corner, trying to figure out why I had lingered for so long, why I had acted so strangely. Of course nothing should surprise me, seeing how I ended up with my arm in a sling…

2.

I wake up like I do most days, way too early, feeling nervous about going to work, not that work is a problem. I am always tense. I turn over, stretch, curl up in a fetal position and try to steal a few more minutes in bed. I remember to breathe deep breaths and it helps the anxieties, but it also wakes me.

I toss. And turn around but nothing works.

I open my eyes just enough to check the time, quickly close them and curl up again. I want to sleep some more, hide a bit longer. It is my fault for going to bed late. I stay up at night for no reason. Watch inane late-night TV until I fall asleep and then in the morning I feel tired, a rut I can't seem to break. I turn to the other side, away from the window and the light, but it does not work. It's my mind. It starts racing before my body is ready to face the day. It starts to worry about the day's outcome and it takes my emotional pulse without asking permission, and as such revs up my anxiety level.

I don't want to go to work today; I should stay home, and call in sick.

I blame my mother. She wanted me to be a teacher and I listened to her.

I don't like thinking about my job, my students or my mother when I first wake up, but I have no choice. My mind goes there automatically. It begins planning lessons, anticipating pitfalls and arguments, figuring the balance between seat work and stand-up teaching. I am not a bad teacher, but I don't think that I am a very good one either, just average and that suits me fine. I don't mind the classroom but I don't like coaching, sponsoring school clubs, or joining committees. I don't raise my hand at staff meetings. I am not one of those popular teachers whose students flock to after school. I am happy not to be noticed and not to be too disliked.

No use fighting it, might as well get up. Staying home makes things worse.

I obsess. I am obsessed with what infects me, mostly about germs and bacteria. I have a fear of hospitals, a popular resort for those invisible parasites.

I am now fully awake, get out of bed, and drag myself to the bathroom. Blind routine is the only way to get through these mornings.

The door of the bathroom is left open. I live alone and as such, privacy is never an issue.

I stand directly in front of the mirror that frames an anxious headshot of myself, head and shoulders caught in a giant life-size passport photo. I don't like looking in the mirror, this one or any other. It is disturbing how this face of mine insists in confronting me every morning, and every morning it irritates me.

My mother installed this mirror and it reminds me of her presence in this house. She is everywhere. We had a fight over me not helping her that day. She did not understand that soccer practice was more important.

My mother took care of all the minor repairs and all the purchases for our home, a house which we had inherited from Aunt Emma, who did not marry and never had any children of her own. Mother was her only relative, her only niece. Aunt died when I was four and I don't remember her very well. I only know her from old photos and from the few things mother has told me about her. My mother, like me, was not one to say much. She was fond of telling me that "a silent mouth is a sweet mouth." She would say that proverb in Gaelic. At the same time she urged me to speak proper English, especially when I mimicked her accent; she asserted that "Canadians don't like people with accents, including the Irish."

My mother worked hard. She was a maid, a cook, and a seamstress for the lodgers who roomed upstairs, lodgers whose room and board allowed us to keep up with the household expenses. She called them lodgers, like her aunt had called them before her and like I got used to calling them, but in effect we were running a boarding house for mostly factory workers, for men who lived alone. Their rent included meals and laundry service. She was a great cook and spent hours in the kitchen. They would praise her *colcannon*, and she would blush. To me it was just mashed potatoes and cabbage with a bit of butter in the middle, a combination that I didn't like. I did love the smell of her soda bread which she baked daily. There were quite a few of these boarding houses in our neighbourhood when I was a child, but they don't exist anymore; we were probably one of the last ones, most having been replaced, and not for the better, by rooming houses owned by absentee landlords. Even that was changing, as families had started to move back into the area.

The lodgers loved mother and saw her as a tireless saint, a real honest-to-goodness martyr, always working, always busy. My mother delighted in cleaning and cooking. Aunt Emma had taught her all the fine points of housekeeping and mom felt indebted to her. The house was spotless and when she was not cooking, her cleaning left the smell of disinfectant everywhere. She also enjoyed being a "businesswoman" and that was the only job she ever had. When we had an empty room mother posted a notice at the small Greyhound Bus station at Queen and Roncesvalles, the one in front of the streetcar loop, but it was mostly through word of mouth that we acquired our guests. We had a good reputation.

The mirror is never kind to me. It always starts the questioning, and I look away.

It's not my face. It has all the right proportions, sym-metrical, with no blemishes. I still have all my hair, and a touch of grey at the temples makes it look even better, as if I had that touch of wisdom that comes with age. I am not unattractive. I eat well; I dislike the taste of sugar, and red meat. I keep away from sodium. I stay in shape. I have very good hygiene; my mother drilled it into me. Maybe too much. I have become, perhaps always was, a bit of a germaphobe and find the need to wash my hands, to keep my body clean, more often than most people. This behaviour may be odd but is not a crime nor is it my real problem. I do have a vice. I smoke, I enjoy smoking cigarettes, and have been a smoker since I quit playing soccer after high school. I have no intentions of giving it up. Smoking relaxes me, helps dispel my anxieties, or at least keep them at bay.

I stare at the mirror. My imperfection is not obvious to people, which is another problem, it might make things easier if it was. Marie might have understood me better.

I met Marie at a Christmas party given by a colleague, a few years after mother died.

"I am a smoker," I tell her apologetically as we appear to have made a connection over a glass of wine, and to get along, "and I hope it's not a put-off."

I like her immediately but already I sound awkward.

"We can't all be perfect," she says, putting me at ease.

"What if we were to kiss?" I say teasingly.

"I assume you have a good supply of mints." She smiles, and I am enamoured.

Sometime later, Marie moved in with me, and all was well for a while.

A couple of months into the relationship, feeling safer than I had ever felt with anyone, and at her urging to be completely honest with each other, I told her about my obsessive fear of germs, and about my immobilizing anxieties.

"What brings them on? Do I make you anxious?"

"No, God no, you don't. They're just there, always have been. They never leave me."

Marie was very sympathetic. She appeared to understand. Of course, I did not tell her the real source of this anxiety. I also told her that I had issues with a silent but domineering mother, and that I had not cried at her funeral. Marie said that I should go to therapy and get professional help right away, that I had waited too long and that a mother must be mourned. She used herself as an example, saying that therapy helped her break the cycle of the abusive relationships she had been in, and added, to lend weight to her argument, that it helped her find me. She smiled when she said that, that smile that I had fallen for when we first met. She loved me and wanted me to be happier, to be problem free. I didn't want to go to therapy. She gently pushed her brand of logic. If I loved her, I would go seek help; if I didn't go see a therapist, it meant that I didn't truly love her. I was stuck. My mother had a proverb for that: "It's hard to make a choice between two blind dogs." And so I chose not to choose and to ignore her advice.

At her insistence, and after months of feeling badgered, I agreed to go see someone; she even gave me names she had gathered from her colleagues.

I made excuses and postponed indefinitely.

"And you call yourself a teacher—I thought that education was about learning and solving problems."
"I never said I was a good teacher."

She didn't like that answer or any of my other explanations. The issue festered until, fed up, she found someone less neurotic, less anxious, less stubborn, and left me. I was both sad and relieved to see her go. Unwilling to move forward, it was easier to live alone.

I look again at myself in the mirror.
You can't really believe that you are happy this way, even living alone.

I stand there longer than I usually do, focused on my eyes, on the face in the mirror, staring straight ahead, using imaginary blinkers and trying hard to internalize that I have to get to work, that this self-flagellation, this talking to myself is useless and won't resolve anything.

Come on, voice what your real problem is, you know you'll feel better.

I find it hard to breathe. The walls are closing in. It is always the same.

"I am not going to see a shrink."

I am very clear on that.

You don't have to go see a shrink, just admit your problem; say it.

The truth is that I know what the problem is, always have, ever since I can remember—no voicing it can make it disappear, no shrink can make it go away. I am stuck with it, and that's the only truth. I know what therapists will say. Their opinions are splashed all over the Internet. There are a few analysts that might take my side, and those are often castigated by their own colleagues. The Internet groups that I follow on sites that deal with these issues are full of examples of real people that have gone through therapy and have wasted their time. It may have prevented a few suicides, and for that I am grateful, but it did not solve the fundamental issues facing them, of that they were very clear, it was unanimous, and I believe them. I am not suicidal, never been tempted, but if I ever am, I will seek help.

"I am not seeing a shrink."

Planted in front of the mirror, I am back to staring at my face, refusing to turn the tap on, refusing to shave, refusing to begin a morning routine that I have followed in this bathroom ever since I was a teenager.

The mirror keeps up the stare, daring me to blink first.

I usually avert my eyes at this point, but not this morning.

I feel a slight twinge on my left side.

You might want to try something different.

"No. I am fine."

You are so obviously not fine.

I open the mirror door to get my razor.

My stone-like face continues to stare me down as the door slowly swings to the right. It opens about a third of the way, and I abruptly stop. I put the razor down.

With my right hand, I partially open the cabinet door and close it. I do it again and again, and again.

I have an idea.

3.

The lowering of my pyjama pants is easy; I grab the elastic edge with my right hand and push them down to the floor until I am able to wiggle out of them, at which point I kick them aside. I do the same for my underwear. My pyjama top is a different story; I first pull at the left sleeve with my right hand, but all I manage to do is stretch the sleeve, and nothing else. I stop for a moment, gather my thoughts, and then grab the top from the front neckline and pull it over my head. I switch and grab the back neckline with the same right hand, yank and drag it downward.

Next, I take out the can of shaving cream, and there I face my first challenge. The cap is on so tight that it is impossible to get it open with one hand. I try and try until it slips from my fingers and crashes to the floor. My left hand wants to help but I stop it in time.

I contemplate not shaving and to grow a beard to make things easier, but quickly dismiss the thought. My routine *has* to stay the same. I make up rules as I go along. There will be no changes to my routine, to my life, and everything has to be like it has always been, *except for the use of this left arm.*

I grab the canister and place it between my thighs, using them as a vise grip, holding on tightly until my right hand easily twists off the cap. I then squirt a big gob of foam directly on my cheek and spread it with my right hand over my face and neck.

It feels unexpectedly good to make decisions, unusual as they may be, and solve these small problems.

I start shaving and stretch the skin by using my face and neck muscles, but not the fingers of my left hand; I keep them tight for the upward thrust of the razor, and loosen them for the way down. By tightening, twisting, and loosening my facial muscles as needed, I am able to get a decent shave, and a good laugh to boot. The distorted expressions I make while shaving are quite funny, and I laugh, something I seldom do.

Like Marie used to remind me, I am mostly incapable of showing overt happiness, or to even be so frivolous as to laugh out loud, even when I thought that something was funny. My mother was a very serious woman, all about work, and not much about contemplating life. "You'll never plough a field by turning it over in your mind," she never tired of repeating as she went about cleaning the house.

I wash off the excess shaving cream with my right hand and towel my face dry. I am now ready for the shower.

As I step into the stall, and before I can turn the water on, the left arm begins to tingle. It already feels strange; unused and limp, it feels heavier. I swing it to stop a mild cramping. I am surprised; I hadn't anticipated the arm fighting back.

Is swinging it using it?

I leave the question unanswered for now. I turn the water on.

Shampooing and moisturizing my hair is a cinch; I pour the liquid directly from the bottle onto my head and massage it easily and thoroughly with the right hand.

It is taking way too long to rinse off the extra foam, all I can do is stand under the nozzle and let the water pressure do its work.

Note to self, pour less.

Soaping my body is another problem; even touching the left arm with the bar of soap feels improper. I have to decide if touching the arm is allowed. It comes down to how easy I want to make this experiment for myself, how honest I want to be. I don't want easy. It must be a complete rejection.

Does it mean not washing it at all?

I will have to decide later. I cringe at the thought of any unwashed parts of my body and at the thought of germs making a home on my skin, even on a disliked left arm. Every time I skipped or forgot to wash my hands before meals, mother would drag me back to the washroom and forcefully scrub them for me. She told me about infections, and how they spread in your body and that people got sick from these infections and parasites and that in some cases they even caused death. I did not want to die. I learned later that she was talking about her own parents who had died, and left her an orphan when she was six. She was raised by her mother's sister in Ireland until unceremoniously shipped to Canada to live with Aunt Emma.

Using my right hand, I soap a washcloth, hang it on the knob of the water faucet and brush the left arm against it by moving my body up and down instead of moving the arm.

I could buy soap with a pump and drip soap on the arm.

That could be construed as washing it.

Not if I just rotate under the water and not move the arm.

It wouldn't get clean. Can someone else wash it?

Sure, as long as it's not me.

I am confusing myself and will need to make those hard decisions when I'm not in such a hurry. I will need to write all this down. The left armpit is fair territory, and almost as if to make up for my distaste for the rest of the arm, I vigorously scrub that area. The right armpit seems impossible to reach with its own hand, but by twisting my right wrist, and holding the soap bar at its edge, I am just able to reach the armpit, enough to rub the soap against it. I raise the arm and the water stream rinses the lathered armpit. To wash the rest of the right arm, I use my mouth to hold a corner of the washcloth and rub it up and down my arm. While doing this, I get soap on my face and in my mouth which is not a good thing, but which also makes me laugh. The worst is when I get soap in my eyes and that stings. I'll learn. Usually I would wash the lower part of my legs and my feet by lifting them up one at a time, but I find that, unable to use my left hand to hold on against the wall, I need to balance on one foot as I wash the other, and that is not an easy task. After many quick attempts, where I keep losing my balance, I'm satisfied that I'm fairly clean. Practice will help. Rinsing is done by rotating side to side until I finally get rid of all the foam. I am more or less happy at the job I have done. I can do better and I know that I will.

I step out of the shower with the left arm dangling to the side.

Using my mouth to hold one corner of the towel in place to dry myself works as well, or almost as well, as if using the left hand to hold it. Other parts of my body are beginning to take over certain functions that previously were done by the left arm. I smile at that too. It is almost automatic, and I find comfort in that. It is almost as if the rest of my body is agreeing with my decision to ignore the left arm and is eager to help.

Brushing my teeth is effortless. Although I usually mouthwash after my morning coffee, I do it now. The child safety cap could have posed a problem but I now know the trick. I again use my thighs to hold the bottle in place and I am easily able to twist the cap off, and rinse.

From now on, please leave the cap on without twisting completely.

I make mental notes to help me later. I will write all of this down when I come home tonight.

I smile like a moron at myself in that stupid little mirror, and laugh again. I also see that my hair needs combing. I do that and smile some more.

Naked, I quickly run to my bedroom, where I slap some aftershave on my face with my right hand. I use the same shaving cream trick I used earlier, and then squirt some cologne on cheeks and chest. The roll-on underarm deodorant is a problem. I can easily do my left armpit but not the right one; unlike the soap, the design of the container makes it more difficult to hold and spread. Arm inwardly bent, monkey-like, elbow up, wrist totally twisted, I rub awkwardly against my right armpit. It more or less works. I will have to switch to a spray, or something that I can manipulate with one hand, maybe a different type of canister.

The socks are easy to put on; the underwear is not a problem. Pants have to be with a zipper, my recent purchase of pants with a button fly will have to go. Buttons are too tricky. Although I can learn.

What about the top?

Let the arm just dangle to the side, or put the arm inside a large sweater and allow the empty sleeve to swing freely while keeping the arm against the chest, or even better, create a makeshift sling and put the arm in it.

I decide on the last choice, the sling will show why I am not using the arm, without having to explain anything. I will have to go from medium to large for all my tops in order to better manage. I'll buy a few, this is just an experiment I remind myself. There is mother's blue silk scarf in the hall closet that I can use as a sling. I had left it there, like I had left untouched most of her things since she died. Tying a knot using my mouth is a cinch. This was her favourite silk scarf, would she have minded if she knew of its use today?

Having the left arm in a sling already feels good.

I pass my mother's room on my way to the front door. I turn the key that protrudes from the lock and peek in. The room is exactly how she had left it the last time she went to St. Joseph's Hospital, more than five years ago. Although I often air it out, the room still smells of old things, of the past, of her, a smell both comforting and discomforting. I close the door and walk out.

4.

As I walk away from my new neighbour, I dig into my school bag and take out a pack of Marlboros. Already open, I shake it gently and use my teeth to pull out a cigarette. I light it without any problems and I am thankful it's not windy. I throw the pack and the lighter back into my bag as I take a deep drag. That first smoke is always so good, but this morning it is even better. I pause for a moment and linger to enjoy it, blowing smoke rings, something I have not done for quite a while. I stare at the blue sky and feel a sense of relief. I look south, down the street, towards the lake. I had forgotten how nice our small street looks in spring. I can see the lake through the trees, a view I take for granted. I spent many days as a kid leaning against the fence on the south side of King Street, overlooking the Gardiner, observing the cars zoom by, and watching the boats on the lake. I was not allowed to cross the bridge and go to the swimming pool or the beach on my own. I remember how this spot was also the perfect place to watch the Canadian National Exhibition Air Show for free. Every Labour Day weekend, the whole neighbourhood would bring their chairs to the fence to watch the show and make a picnic of it. Some staked out a space on the bridge that linked King Street and the lake to have a clearer view. My mother would never join us, she was too busy for such frivolity. Sometimes the lodgers would come and stand with me. She hated the noise of the airplanes, and could not wait until the air show was over. Her seriousness was another unwanted characteristic she passed on to me, along with her inability to get close to anyone. I tried to do what she expected from me, to be a good son and not upset her. I am not sure how much of it was that she didn't love me, as if I was a burden she hadn't asked for, or how much of it was that she didn't know how to express her love, any love, because of what she had been through and the death of her parents at a young age. Nevertheless, leaning against the barrier and looking at the lake always soothed my anxieties and helped me forget about my mother.

I would generally walk to work, but today I am going to be at least 20 minutes late for my first class if I don't take public transit. I don't mind teaching at Parkdale Collegiate, it was my old high school before it became a collegiate. None of my former teachers were still there when I first transferred, which was good. It was somehow comforting to be close to home, as if I needed that extra security. After a while, the novelty wore off and it just became a place of work.

There is a streetcar every few minutes at this time of the morning and as such I am not too worried. I should also phone the school and let them know that I am going to be late. At least I have a reason, a visible one. With the cigarette dangling to the side of my mouth, I take out my cellphone and click on the school number. I'm surprised at how easy I can manage with one arm, one hand. The streetcar stops in front of me. I quickly hang up before the phone rings, throw out my cigarette and put the phone away as I climb on.

On the streetcar, walking past students that I recognize but who I have not taught, I move to the back and find a seat. The students acknowledge my presence with a nod of the head and I do the same thing.

I lean against the window. The arm, tight against my chest, is at rest, but still feels heavy and stiff. I'm already tired and the day has barely begun.

I think back on my morning.

What a strange little woman, that neighbour. She seemed so happy and friendly, maybe too happy, maybe not all there. Probably just fishing for information like most new neighbours tend to do. There was a look of uncertainty that peeked through her perkiness, but maybe it's just me, I tend to unsettle people, I'm awkward around people. The rattle of the streetcar lulls me to sleep and although it is only three stops to my destination, I allow myself to close my eyes.

I am not sure that I am doing the right thing with this experiment.

Very much like the relationship with my mother, I have always had a disconcerting feeling about this arm. I became aware that something wasn't right around grade four.

I like gym. It is a break from spelling and math. We are now old enough to go to gym every day, and I like that very much. We learn new games, sometimes we run, other times we try climbing ropes, which I am not very good at, and sometimes we pass the ball around. Today, we are standing in a circle, taking turns throwing a ball the size of a small basketball to each other. It should be easy to catch, it's not a difficult thing. The ball comes to me, my right arm goes up to catch it, but my left arm takes a little bit longer to go up and so I drop the ball. I look around. No one laughs. Jim brags very loudly that he can catch it with one hand and he does. When the ball gets closer to me, I get set. I watch the ball fly through the air, keep my eyes on it, try not to blink; my right arm is ready but again my left arm refuses to listen. I am telling it to go up faster and faster but, as if on purpose, it moves even slower. I graze the ball with my right hand but can't hold on. Jim, and Fred, his best friend, laugh at me. I try to ignore them, but I get nervous, anxious, and worry about my next turn. I feel sick to my stomach. It gets worse as the ball gets closer, I feel like I am going to throw up. I resist the urge and try one more time.

I don't know what is going on; the ball gets to me and I drop it. I feel like crying. And now it's not just Jim and Fred who laugh but some of the others too. I get angry, and I tell my left arm to help me. I say please.

Mr. Brown, our gym teacher, repeats his encouragement, "Don't worry, Jack; you'll catch it next time." I don't. The ball comes to me and I drop it again. I hear the whole class laughing, and I run out of the gym.

The loud voices of teenagers startle me and jar me out of that past. I remember that day vividly, mostly the feeling of utter humiliation, a feeling that over time has morphed into an ever present dull pain.

The teens are noisy, showing off for each other, lacing theirs arguments with profanities. One of my students, a nice kid, although not a very strong student, waves at me and I wave back.

I close my eyes again, try to savour a few more moments of not having to deal with the life I have created for myself, a career my mother had suggested and that I followed without asking too many questions. I had never really wanted to be a teacher, I would have liked to do something with sports, maybe broadcasting or sports journalism. She said that I was silly, that those were not professions, and that teaching would be a fine career. I went along.

The streetcar stops, the doors open, the students fight their way out, the door closes. I stay glued to my seat, unable to follow them down the steps of the streetcar and to the school entrance.

I don't even pretend to get up.

As the streetcar pulls away, a few of the students look back, surprised that I didn't get off. I can't, I just can't face anyone this morning. I need some time to think. I will call the school later, use the arm as an excuse, and tell them that I am going to the doctor, an emergency. If necessary, I'll have Celeste, the school secretary, get a supply teacher for me, she'll do that without asking too many questions, she likes me. I'll make up something as to why I didn't call earlier. I lean back against the window and it feels good. I start to fall asleep again.

5.

Every stop is a jolt and every jolt shakes a sore and cramping left arm, and inflicts pain. I take it out of the sling and swing it, unsure if I am allowed to do this, but grateful for the respite.

I recognize every corner of this neighbourhood and every building much, much too well. I have never strayed too far from this old village of Parkdale—then when I was a child, and now when I know better. I have used the area between Lake Ontario and Queen Street, between High Park and the CNE grounds as my personal corner of the world. My mother liked to pretend that we lived in a real village and to her, Parkdale was Toronto.

The streetcar passes Dufferin and the eastern edge of my small world. I find it difficult to keep my eyes open and enjoy the freedom of being half awake, when I should be fully awake and standing in front of a classroom, teaching English to a restless group of grade nine students.

My mother was a difficult woman to understand, she didn't say much in terms of explaining life or questioning her surroundings, she survived for the most part on rules and proverbs. She only seemed happy when doing housework, when taking care of the lodgers. She did make great stews, which were very much appreciated on those cold days when I would come home for lunch, frozen to the bone. Fern Public School was seven blocks away. The winds coming from the lake were frigid and made the winters worse. I liked her thick stew with oversized pieces of carrots and chunky potatoes, which you could smell as soon as you opened the front door.

Of course she never said anything, but I have a feeling that mother never forgave me for being the cause of her being shipped to Canada. She arrived to Aunt Emma's four months pregnant and without a husband. My friends had fathers, and bragged about them, but not me. He was not to be talked about. She explained that he was not important, that he was a nobody. When I insisted that she tell me something, anything, she said that he disappeared when he found out that she was pregnant, that in the end he was a coward like all men, that she made a mistake in trusting what she thought was a kind, gentle, man. *Malarkey.*

"It's the quiet pigs that eat the grain. And don't you forget that," she said.
"Is he still alive?"

She said she didn't know nor did she care whether he was dead or alive, that he was a dishonourable man, a *bradach*, not like the people from Cork, the men of her native city. As far as she was concerned, he was dead and I should think of him in the same way. She would not discuss it any further and she didn't. At least I knew that he was Irish, not from Cork, and a quiet man.

There was a time that I thought the arm didn't like me because I didn't have a father, that this was a punishment, a curse of some sort. Two parents, two arms, one parent, one good arm. In some ways and for some reason, that thought was comforting. I was not to blame; my cowardly father was to blame for my arm's insubordination. Since my mother didn't care, I told my school friends that he died in a motorcycle accident in Dublin, before I was born. I am not sure why the motorcycle or Dublin, I guess it sounded more tragic and they could never be able to check the veracity of the story. The kids at Fern still didn't like me, I was one of the few Irish Catholics in the school, not that I ever felt very "Oirish," as my mother would pronounce it, or Catholic. But then, kids picked on anyone that was different and I was different.

The streetcar continues its journey along Queen Street and I am not sure where I am going. I get off after I see St. Michael's Hospital. I had gone far enough, crossed into the east end, a foreign neighbourhood, ironically where the Irish had settled when they first came to Canada—mostly Protestants at first, Catholics like Aunt Emma came later. She had chosen to stay away from both. My mother said that Aunt Emma could have lived in Peterborough, where most of the immigrants from Cork had gone, but she was stubbornly independent and chose to live with the English in Parkdale. I think it was more about the economics of running a boarding house in the right location. My mother often confused me but never as much as when talking about her Irish roots. Mother would be quick to dump on both Protestants and Catholics, cursing their endless war. And yet, at the same time, she cooked mostly Irish dishes and would listen to The Chieftains when the lodgers were at work. The worst was when she played some of Aunt Emma's old Irish laments. I still remember "The Town I Loved So Well" and "Four Green Fields." I didn't understand how she only had bad things to say about the Irish, yet everything she did was a reminder that we were Irish, down to the trinkets on her dresser and her shamrock earrings.

I look for a place to get a coffee and to wash my right hand—streetcars are full of germs and I had touched a number of things without being careful. I use my sleeve whenever I can but this morning I had been careless and had touched the back of a seat with my bare hand.

There is a Starbucks at the corner and I am thankful for their clean washrooms. Letting the water run over my right hand, I almost give in to the temptation of putting the left hand under the water, to also clean it. I resist. To mitigate the cramping, I take the arm out of the sling and let it hang at my side. There, it feels a bit better. I'll find a solution for the dirt and grime that may be accumulating on it. The idea of uncleanliness makes me cringe but I need to continue this experiment. It is important that I succeed. I hold the sling open and the arm goes in without me having touched it. And yet I realize that the act of going into the sling is controlled by me and thus I am still communicating with it. I can't do that again, I need to find a better way and be stronger about not using it.

Sitting on a park bench, the cramping is manageable, the anxieties at bay. The Marlboros help. Relaxing, I blow ever larger smoke rings in the air and take sips of the coffee. I should phone the school and let them know that I am hurt, that I have gone to the doctor or somewhere. I will later, after I finish my cigarette. They'll understand, I have an excuse. I would be in my spare period now anyway, which means they won't need to use an on-call teacher and that I am fine until lunch time. I can relax a bit longer. They will see for themselves when I go back. I am not one to miss work, another thing my mother drilled into me.

I watch the people going by, most walking at a brisk pace, having somewhere to go. I don't want to go anywhere. It is the first time in a very long while that I have broken from routines and it feels good. I light another cigarette and take a sip. Coffee and a cigarette, and not having to face students, add to this perfect sunny day. I stare ahead of me, letting the people come in and out of my peripheries rather than having my eyes or my head follow them.

My cellphone rings

It is the school, probably Celeste. I let it ring until it goes to voice mail. I'll explain when I get there. I don't want to talk to anyone right now. I close my eyes while I smoke. I am tired. The latte from Starbucks, ordered extra hot, burns as it goes down, the smoke does the same, and somehow they each make the other taste better.

Time slows down.

A homeless man asks for change. I fumble to give him a few coins. I don't have much, wish I had more.

"God bless," he says, as he walks away.

"Thank you." I accept his blessing, it can't hurt.

My mother said that I was too anxious for my own good.

"Jack, YOU are an anxious lad, my son. Everything is not about you."

Of course, she was right, but I had reasons to be anxious. If the arm had behaved more like a normal arm, I wouldn't have been so anxious. If I had a father, I wouldn't have been so anxious. If my mother hugged me more, I wouldn't have been so anxious. If she had talked to me more, explained herself, shared her story, I wouldn't have been so anxious. If I had real friends, I wouldn't have been so anxious.

I take a deep breath. Feeling sorry for myself. That was not allowed in my house, my mother said it was a sign of weakness; you accept life as it comes.

"You must take the little potato with the big potato."

It seemed that all I ever got in life were the small potatoes.

A young couple sits on a bench across from me. With ease, the man puts his left arm around his girlfriend's shoulder. The young woman reminds me of Paula, I wonder what happened to her, what she looks like now… of course, she would be my age and unlike this young lady in front of me.

Paula was the most beautiful girl at Fern Public School. We were in the same elementary class. We weren't friends and didn't really talk to each other at that time.

Later, the smart kids went to Humberside and the rest of us went to Parkdale Secondary for grade nine. Out of familiarity, and out of feeling a bit lost in that first year of high school, we said "hi" to each other as we passed through the halls. In grade ten, she was in my math class, and I couldn't tire of looking at her. Paula became popular and had a lot of friends, but she would still say "hi" and wave to me. She came to watch the school soccer games with her girlfriends and I would see her there on the sidelines. It encouraged me to play harder, secretly dedicating to her any goals I scored. She was in music and I took a greater interest when the orchestra played in the auditorium, sneaking away from my class assigned area and into a front seat. I became good at soccer. She became good at everything, and unlike me, made the honours list. In grade eleven, I was a starter on the senior team, and the coach understood that I didn't do throw-ins. He didn't care—by that point I could score regularly. My feet took over where the left arm failed me. I am not sure if people noticed that I ran a bit strangely, that the left arm did not swing as freely as the other, but no one said anything as long as I scored.

In my last year, after winning the Ontario finals, and feeling quite confident, I asked Paula out on a date. It seemed that everyone except me was dating by that time.

I still remember how she looked the day I asked her out. She had short black hair, recently cut, spiky. Her face and long legs had a light brown tan, which was accentuated by a short blue dress. She was so beautiful and I was so nervous. She said "yes" and that made me ecstatic, happier than I had ever felt. A joy that came from deep inside of me, swelling to the surface every time I thought of Paula and our upcoming date. I ran home that day, stopping long enough to remind myself that she said yes, barely able to contain myself, marveling at how lucky I was. Of course, I didn't tell my mother, I just told her I had to go to a soccer practice, she didn't question it. I don't think she cared. By this point she was very busy with her business of keeping the lodgers clean and well-fed, and I was old enough to take care of myself. It didn't matter to me, I was truly happy for the first time in my life, more thrilled than when playing soccer and scoring goals.

I am waiting for Paula in front of Mac's Milk, a convenience store not far from her house. She lives a block north of Queen Street, on Grafton Avenue, close to Roncesvalles, in the Polish neighbourhood. Although I know her house, I have to wait here at the corner; her father does not like her dating anyone, let alone someone who is not from their community. I see her turn the corner and she waves, her trademark little shake of the hand, arm straight to her side.

"Do you want an ice cream?"

We walk into the store and she gets a strawberry cream delight. I get a chocolate Popsicle.

We walk towards the lake.

"Can I have a taste of yours?"

Of course I let her.

She is beautiful.

She smiles and offers me hers. I lick where her tongue has been and that makes me feel all strange, tingly, and even more anxious than usual.

Along the Queensway towards High Park, we walk past the streetcar garage beside the loop and St. Joseph Hospital. There are several entrances to the park for cars and for people, but we take a shortcut along a path that starts right at the edge of where the houses are, and that cuts through the trees on an angle.

I take her right hand in mine as we go up the hill. It feels strange to hold someone's hand. I don't remember holding anyone's hand, not even my mother's. Paula says that she doesn't date too much and that if her father knew that she was here with me, he would kill her. She is supposed to be out with her girlfriend. I say that I am supposed to be playing soccer. We both laugh. I tell her that it is my first date, and that I am nervous. She kisses me on the cheek to put me at ease. I think that she likes me. She tells me that she has gone on a few secret dates before but nothing serious since she is not allowed to have a real boyfriend. I kiss her back, on the cheek, as we walk side by side. I am happy. I think that she is glad to be with me. We could be boyfriend and girlfriend, secretly of course.

She tells me that her father has old-fashioned ideas like most Polish immigrants, and she can't wait until she is old enough to leave home.

She asks, "Where do you want to go?"

"I don't know, wherever you want to go."

She leads me. She probably expects to make out at some point, and I get butterflies in my stomach thinking about it.

I worry that I may not do it right. I have never made out before.

I am more nervous than usual. Maybe my mother is right. I don't want to think about my mother. It's just that I want to act normal, to be like the other boys Paula has dated. I worry as to when the right time will be to put my arm around her, and the right time to kiss her on the lips, maybe touch her breasts and do other stuff. I get both excited and terrified thinking about it. I don't even know if she will let me put my hand under her blouse. I won't know what to do with her bra. I'm a mess.

We take another path towards the pond, one that leads to bushes and tall grass. I kiss her on the cheek again as we walk, she blushes and gives me a quick peck on the lips. We laugh. I do the same, closed lips, closed eyes. I shouldn't worry so much. I feel like I have never felt before, like my chest is going to explode. We sit on the grass to rest, she is to my left and we stare straight ahead. We can see the lake and the pond from where we are.

"*Look, a sailboat.*"

We talk about our teachers, the ones we like and those that we don't. It feels good to be out with a girl, to be normal. She wants to go to the University of Toronto and I regret not having studied very hard, my marks barely acceptable for York University. She could really be my girlfriend. She talks about music, I talk about sports. She likes playing the cello, I like playing soccer. We agree that we are kind of the same.

I start to worry about my next move.

As soon as she finishes talking about her girlfriend who is now dating a boy older than her, I will put my arm around her, draw her to me and kiss her on the lips and make out. Simple as that.

She stops talking. I am trembling.

I think I am lifting my arm to hug her, but the arm doesn't move. It doesn't even pretend to be moving. It stays anchored to the ground, unwilling to do what I tell it. Paula is waiting patiently, looking straight ahead at the lake. I try again. Stuck to the ground, the arm refuses to go towards Paula's shoulder; the left hand refuses to touch her. The arm refuses to hold her, to squeeze her towards me, to make me happy. I am fighting with myself in silence. I tell the arm to move or else, I swear I'll kill it. I plead with it to please listen to me, it doesn't. I am mortified that Paula might notice my struggles. I turn my head away. I am so embarrassed. I feel myself blushing. I don't know what to do. My bad anxieties take over. I am paralyzed.

Paula puts her hand on my knee while still looking straight ahead. She is trying to tell me that it is okay, that she is fine with me putting my arms around her. I want so badly to do that. My stomach is in knots. I try again with the left arm, and the arm feels like it weighs a ton. It's a nightmare and I give up.

We stay like that for a while watching the sailboats in the distance. I try to hide my anger.

Paula does not notice what I am going through, but after a few more minutes she says, "Let's go see the animals."

I am almost relieved.

"Sure." My voice trembles.

She is not angry, more like disappointed I would guess. I don't know. I am so angry at myself for letting the arm win, that I don't see clearly, that I can't think. I just want to cry. She must sense that there is something wrong, but she doesn't say anything, holds my right hand and leads me to the small zoo in the park.

"Look, a buffalo." She points.

A peacock struts its tail and it would be quite beautiful if I was not so mad.

We talk about the different animals and after a while she asks if we can go home so that she doesn't get in trouble.

I walk her back to the Mac's store in silence.

She says, "Thanks for the ice cream, I had a good time," and kisses me on the cheek.

On Queen Street, livid, I wait until she turns the corner and I bang my left arm against a lamppost. And against the next one, and the next one.

6.

I decide not to go back to school and make my way home instead. I also, and uncharacteristically, choose not to phone the school and explain myself. I turn the corner and walk south on Wilson Park. That date with Paula was probably the worst day of my life—not probably, for sure. Paula did ask me a week later if I wanted to go out with her to see a movie. I made an excuse and avoided her from that point on. I didn't really date after that for a long while, I started smoking instead. I also quit soccer. Didn't see the purpose. I realized the idea of becoming a professional soccer player was childish. My mother had never cared if I played or not, she never realized that I played in part so that she could see that I was a normal boy, so that I might get some accolades from somewhere. Normality for her was having a career, finding a wife and having children, in that order. My marks weren't very high but I did get in at York University, and despite the insane commute, I persevered and became a teacher.

I tried being sociable in university, and at first, to ease my nervousness, I went out in mixed groups. I was afraid that on a one-on-one date, I would be discovered as being unusual, odd. My mother was a teetotaller, and to annoy her I grew to enjoy Guinness and to at least live up to one of the Oirish characteristics she warned me against. Going to bars on and off campus and drinking for a couple of hours helped me overcome some of my anxieties. I found that women liked my Irish accent, which I trotted out when sufficiently drunk. I hid the drinking from my mother, or at least I thought that I did. She didn't care what I did outside of the house, as long as I didn't do it at home and jeopardize the wholesome reputation of our business. Sneaking in drunk through the back door became a common recurrence for a while. Mother once asked if I had a girlfriend and given any thoughts about marriage, children. I said no. She never asked again, except that she did remind me that I still wasn't allowed to bring women to the house unless I had proposed first. Thankfully, she quickly forgot about it, busying herself with the running of the household for our five semi-permanent lodgers residing on the second and third floors of our big house. I was on my own and it had its advantages. I went on more dates and learned that as long as I had a few drinks, used my right arm and right hand, I could have a quasi-normal liaison with women, even able to be intimate and make furtive love at their places. None of those encounters compared to what I had felt with Paula, and until I met Marie much later, I had to admit that all my relationships were a wreck. I secretly hoped to meet Paula again, somewhere and by chance, to explain to her what had happened, but since she had moved out of the neighbourhood, I never saw her again.

I spot Lisa as I get closer to our houses.

I stomp out the cigarette that I was smoking and cross the street.

She is on her knees, her head in one of the rose bushes that separate the walkways to our two houses, and run the length of the front yards, all the way from the porches to the sidewalk. Our houses are the only two properties on the street that are free from the towering, mature trees that populate the whole neighbourhood.

She lifts her head at the last moment, just as I turn into my walkway.

"Hi, neighbour," she says in that same loud and cheerful voice with which she greeted me this morning. She looks genuinely happy to see me, but I bet she is like that with everyone, part of the nursing, bringing people back to health, making people feel good, uniform.

Lisa reminds me of a sunflower, or a lollipop. With that small, tiny body, and that very round face perched on top, she is a bit odd looking, but likeable, I can see how her warmth could be infectious and how she would be a good nurse.

"Hi, Lisa," I answer.

She had been tending the newly planted rose garden, attempting to bring some colour to that narrow and weedy grass patch that acts as a border between the two houses. It is something she had started last fall without asking, not that she had to ask, the grass strip was mostly on her side. She had removed the plastic covering that had shielded the rose bush from the harsh winter, trimming the stems and tilling by hand the earth around it. Watching her bare hands touching the dirt gives me goosebumps, she should wear garden gloves. Dirt and germs get under your fingernails and it's hard to get them out. Nevertheless, I am the one with the problem, not her.

Staying on her knees, she pats the newly poured black dirt. She is wearing red shorts, and I notice the surprising whiteness of her legs; her bare knees are stained by bits of green and brown from the grass and dirt. She obviously has no issues with getting grimy.

"You are home early, not feeling good? The arm?" she continues in a familiar tone, as if she has known me forever.

I see the perfectly shaped circle of new soil at the base of each rose bush. I can also see down her white blouse, and she is not wearing a bra. I get closer and as she bends a bit lower to remove a weed, I see most of one small breast and a partially visible tattoo underneath it. My libido had been dormant for so long that I am surprised at the stirring between my legs, the more so since I wasn't physically attracted to her.

Inking is another phenomenon that I don't understand, but more and more people are getting tattoos, including many of my young students. I would never put ink on myself. Lisa pushes some of the dirt against the base of the roses, pressing down on the earth. She must be unaware that the two undone top buttons are revealing much more than she might have wanted to show. I feel like a pervert.

I look away from Lisa's tattoo.

She lifts her head.

"Did you go see a doctor?"

And maybe it is because I am not sure as to what to do once I go inside the house, or more likely, that I want to stay and surreptitiously take another look at her uncovered breasts and the tattoo, that I linger on my front yard, and talk to a neighbour, to a stranger.

On her knees she shuffles to the next rose bush and I follow her.

"I didn't go to the doctor, I'm OK, just didn't feel well enough to stay at work. I guess I'm skipping… but I kind of have an excuse."

She straightens up, adjusts her glasses and smears the lenses as she pushes them back against her nose. Not sexy at all, but quite innocent. She is a waif compared to Marie and the few women I have dated since university. She looks fragile, like she could easily break, although her tattoo indicates otherwise, unless she just followed the trend.

"Skipping hey, boy are you setting a bad example for your students…"

She laughs to let me know that she is kidding.

"And you, skipping too?"

"It's my day off, four on, four off, been working the day shifts, twelve hours each, noon to midnight, and I am taking advantage of the beautiful sunny day to do some pruning and some planting. Is it OK that I planted these here—I know it's close to the property line?"

I notice that she has combed her hair and is wearing lipstick, light pink. It suits her, I am almost tempted to tell her, but I am sure that although new at this, that's not what neighbours say to each other.

My arm is cramping again, I need to lie down and rest, take some painkillers, but I stay.

"I wish I could do that in teaching, four days on, four days off, but twelve hours with students, can you imagine…" I let the sentence trail off and make a face. I can't believe I am having my second neighbourly chat with someone I have avoided for six months.

And she laughs.

I like that I made her laugh. It is a warm laugh, unadulterated, full of joy, and so I laugh with her. She gets up, moves to the next rose bush and empties the remaining black compost from the heavy plastic bag. I follow her and when she gets down on her knees to work the dirt, I look again at her partially exposed dangling breasts and can see the tattoo a bit better now. It looks like a small heart in red, right between her breasts, although there is more of it that I can't see. And again, I feel something stirring.

"I should help," I say, and get closer.

"No, I am fine. Thanks. Besides, your arm… I am sorry, I am taking so much of your time. You probably need to go in and rest, take some Advil, the arm has to be cramping by now."

I wonder for a moment how she knows that it is cramping and then remember that she is a nurse. I get the feeling that she doesn't mind me talking to her, and I surprisingly oblige.

"It's OK. I am happy to be out on this beautiful day and not in school. Don't worry; I don't have much to do, except some marking, and that can wait." And I give a small, silly laugh. Very different from hers—mine is dishonest. It has to do with feigning interest so that I can look down her blouse and forget the pain of the cramping arm.

"You're bad… " she giggles, "my partner is kind of in the same business, you know, education, but he isn't a teacher."

Lisa tells me that her partner is an administrator at Humber College, the Lakeshore Campus not far from here, on the Queensway, where the old mental asylum used to be. He is in HR and helps students find jobs after they get their degrees. She proudly divulges how successful he is at finding these new graduates work in their fields, how rewarding it is after the long hours he puts in.

She putters around the rose bush while talking and I listen to her, positioning myself accordingly.

Lisa almost catches me looking when she lifts her head.

"He really likes helping students," she repeats.

"That's great."

I ask her about her job. She tells me that she works in the palliative care unit, and that it is stressful, emotional, but that she is used to it.

"I think nursing is so important in our society. People like you are worth their weight in gold." I believe what I just said, but I also agree with my mother about men being pigs and I am a prime example.

Lisa smiles at the compliment and continues to tell me that her work is part social worker, part nurse, part physiotherapist.

"Physiotherapist?"

She says that some of her patients are not very mobile and that they need to be moved, turned around, and massaged or they will get bed sores.

"Some are unable to bathe themselves and so we have to do it for them, help them."

I get a sudden idea and reject it as quickly.

"It sounds physically challenging as well as emotionally stressful." I am being honest, I remember how hard the nurses worked and how they helped my mother in her dying days. No matter what my feelings towards my mother were, I didn't like seeing her suffer.

"I like helping people. Well, I feel lucky compared to what they are going through. I am sorry, I am babbling on, go in and rest that arm of yours. And please don't be shy, let me know if I can be of any help." And she points to my arm.

"By the way, Lisa, you are doing great with those bushes. Thanks for taking care of this strip of grass. It's never looked better."

She smiles and winks at me. I have never understood winkers, the act lacked subtlety, but I accept it as part of her innocence, her friendliness.

I walk to my door and leave her to tend to her flowers.

I must admit that she didn't look too bad, much better than this morning when she wore that baggy sweatshirt that did nothing for her, except to accentuate her overly round head. She is almost cute when she takes care of herself. Her hair down instead of in a ponytail frames her face in a more youthful way, makes her look less round, prettier. Even more importantly, she sounded like a person one could trust. Not a woman I would want to date, but someone I would want as a friend, if I wanted friends.

I get to my door, put the key into the lock, leave it there, turn around, and go back to her.

"Lisa, can you do me a favour?"

7.

I startle her. Lisa jumps back, a look of fear in her eyes. I am sorry for being so stupid, and can only imagine what kind of crazy, excited expression she sees on my face. She quickly recovers and has a big smile when she sees that it's me, "You scared me, Jack." I feel better as she goes back to being normal. She has that same ability that Marie had at the beginning of our relationship, an ability to put me at ease with a word, a gesture, a tone, a smile. I needed that in a woman, in a friend—my mother did the opposite. She unwittingly did a great job of fuelling my anxieties.

"Sorry, didn't mean to…"

She laughs at her own jitters, and very warmly asks, "Don't worry, I frighten easily. What can I do you for, Jack?"

She sounds like we are the best of friends when this is only our third conversation, our first real meeting, and it emboldens me. I keep my eyes on her eyes, hesitate for a split second and then go for it.

"You are a nurse, right? Then I guess it's kind of a nursing question."

"Shoot."

"Lisa, this is going to sound strange, but I need someone to help me, and you can say no, I won't get offended. I don't know who else to ask, I don't have many close friends, well none really…"

"You don't mean that."

I ignore what is another painful issue of mine. Seriously, how could I have developed a sense of friendship, when my mother frowned on my bringing home any school friends? She said it wouldn't be fair to the lodgers, some of whom had night shifts. She said friends come and go, you can't rely on them; you should only rely on yourself. I obeyed her, everything about the lodgers was more important than me. They put a roof over our heads and food on our table, she was fond of saying. She said things with such certainty that you didn't dare contradict her. The reality is that I didn't have any real friends then, and I don't have any now. I have colleagues and vague acquaintances.

"I thought that because you are a nurse you would understand. It's a bit strange. What I am about to tell you may even surprise you, so stop me at any point, if you don't want to hear, stop me any time…"

I jabber, of course, that is what I do when I am nervous. She stands up and I am glad, it makes it easier to talk and I am not tempted to look down her blouse.

"If it is that strange, I am not sure I am the right person."

She suddenly looks worried and a bit fearful. I wonder if she is regretting her friendliness.

"OK, I understand, sorry, I won't bother you again."

She looks at me intensely but my timidity or my blush, that I can feel getting worse by the second, works in my favour.

"No, go ahead, you have piqued my curiosity. How bad can it be?"

And she chuckles. She is always smiling and laughing but it is quite innocent, or maybe she is just nervous all the time, much like me with my anxieties. People manifest theirs differently.

"You are going to think that I am crazy, but I have a problem, not serious, but still… a problem."

I had meant to simply tell her about the experiment, without telling her too much about my antagonistic feelings towards the arm, but I instantly realize that it would be silly and that she would eventually find out. So, unlike with Marie, I decide to tell her everything. She listens attentively and nods as I explain the issue about the left arm. I minimize the severity, lest she thinks that I am a total freak. Her face takes on a mixture of seriousness and incredulity as I divulge my plan to disconnect myself from the arm. I sound crazier as I voice it to a stranger, worse, to a neighbour, and I suddenly regret having started this whole conversation.

"Do you want me to stop? I am sorry." I hope she does stop me.

She doesn't want me to, and I continue. I explain that I am just trying something different, that it is a simple experiment and only for a couple of weeks, that I am trying to prove a point to modern therapy. A psychological or physiological experiment, if you will. I am not sure myself as to what it is. I tell her that I will write an article about the whole experience, help others like me, and start a blog.

I fumble, not as sure as I was when I first got the idea to ask her.

"It sounds like… a… body disorder thing… didn't think… it affected men."

"Not really, it's just a small problem that I have."

I don't want her to think that I have a full-blown condition, and I also don't want to tell her that I know quite a bit about Body Image Disorders and even Body Integrity Identity Disorder, which one might think is what I have, but it is not. I have read all that there is to read about it. I know the debate. I belong to a small group on the Internet, well, not really belong, I just read their posts, I don't participate much except to support them. What I have learned is that there are all kinds of people with various degrees of this disorder. I should explain to Lisa that I am at the low end, but I am certain she would misunderstand, I know what doctors think and I know what those with the issues are saying.

I am not sure why am I trusting this neighbour. Is it the nurse thing, the breast thing, the tattoo thing, the being nice thing? I can't be sure. But instead of ending whatever this was and just going home, I carry on.

"… Because of… in the spirit of the experiment, washing my arm and hand, even dangling it under the water is against… I admit that I am a bit of a germaphobe, well, more than a bit… would mean that I am still paying attention to it, you understand… that I'm directing… which I can't… the experiment, you know… someone who lives nearby… I am stuck…"

I can't stop babbling and she doesn't stop me, she just listens and so I am forced to continue.

"… My armpit, the right one… once a day… you… what I mean, as a nurse, I thought…"

She looks at me intently, as if to see if I am playing her and if I really mean what I am saying, what I am asking of her. I repeat that, fail or succeed, it would make a great article. I would mention her help, give her credit if she wanted. I drone on.

She finally gets a few words in.

"This is much more than I can handle. This is, pardon me for saying, but… a job… for a therapist."

I knew that is what people would say, which is why I don't talk to people about it. Although I am far too invested in this conversation to stop now. I ignore what she just said.

"Never mind the issue, but the experiment… the point is that the arm is getting dirty, will get worse, the hand is probably full of germs already, and I need someone to wash it. I know it's… it's just about washing the arm, the hand, it's not a big deal."

She smiles, pauses, thinks about it, but ultimately shakes her head.

"No, no, I don't think so. I am sorry, I can't help you, Jack. I don't think it would be appropriate. I am out of my league on this one. Thomas would not understand it, and would not like it, he's jealous enough as it is. To be honest, I am not even sure I understand, and I am a nurse. These are issues beyond my expertise. I also don't even know you that well; until today, I had the feeling you were avoiding us, me. Sorry, Jack."

8.

I had misjudged her as much as she had misunderstood me. I had thought from her friendliness that we were becoming friends, more than just neighbours; of course, the reality is that I had just met her. It was not her, it was me. I was the strange one, I was the one who knew nothing about friendships. She was also worried about what Thomas, her husband, her partner, would think, and that I can understand. He would suspect there was more to it, look how much I enjoyed looking down her blouse. He would know that guys are scum and take advantage of friendly women. My mother attested to that. The reality is that one minute I don't like to talk to neighbours and the next minute I look down a neighbour's blouse, get turned on, tell her that I am a freak and would she please come to my house and wash my fucking arm. And then, lo and behold I am surprised that she says no and looks at me as if I am a madman. I am hurt by her rejection, I am a total idiot, that's what I am. My mother was right; I'm a bit strange in the head. I hadn't been able to convey that the experiment was one issue and the washing of the arm was another. I had muddled the discourse.

I go to the kitchen sink and wash my right hand. My cellphone rings again, and it's the same number that has been calling all day, my school. This is not the time. I let it go to voicemail. They'll have gotten a supply teacher for the afternoon by now. I'll call later before the secretary leaves for the day. I'll explain, and go to work tomorrow, forget about all this nonsense, the arm, the neighbour, everything.

But, I must admit to feeling hurt and rejected, even though I knew deep down inside that it was perhaps indelicate for me to even ask. I really should think twice before I speak to people.

It's way past lunch time, and I have nothing in the house.

What hurt as much as the rejection is the incredulous look she gave me when I got to a certain point in my story, that glare where I could sense she thought I might be crazy, that I might have crossed a line. It was the same look my mother gave me the few times I mentioned my struggles with the arm. Which is why I never told anyone else. I should have learned my lesson.

And now I feel bad again, like I had done something wrong. The old feelings of guilt and shame are back even stronger. The truth is that I *had* done something wrong, I had talked to a neighbour and continued the conversation beyond a simple "Good morning," a mistake I will not make again.

I am sure I can hire someone to wash my arm. Plenty of people would do that for money. It was stupid of me to ask a neighbour. What was I thinking? All that friendliness, laughing and smiling, all that nursing care fooled me. I guess I thought that if she accepted to wash my arm it would have shown some understanding for what I am going through. I couldn't have risked that with a colleague at work; at least this way, I could just go on ignoring the neighbour and act as if nothing happened. I had made a mistake.

I will hire a home care nurse. It is best not to get involved with people that are close by. Make it a business transaction— that's how my mother treated the lodgers, she never got too close, except maybe for one, and that didn't work out.

I once read a play of Beckett's in university where the main character says something like, "The mistake one makes is to speak to people." I don't remember what or whom he was referring to, but today it would certainly apply to me. I renew my resolution not to speak to people.

I check that Lisa is gone before venturing outside in search of something to eat.

Left arm in the sling, I light a cigarette and head north to Queen Street. There are so few restaurants or stores on King Street that I avoided it. I have done this uphill walk my whole life, I could do it blindfolded. I look at the trees that were already tall when I was a kid, but are now gigantic. That majestic evergreen two doors up reached the second storey windows of Mrs. Best's house when I was young, and it now soars above the roof of her tall three-storey house.

I can't get Lisa out of my head. People don't understand and why would they? I made myself feel bad, she had nothing to do with it. I am also not very good at explaining what I have. Some days it feels one way and other days it feels different. I know there is a label for what I experience. What if what I have is different than that label, what if it is a simple war between me and the arm? What if I am not a case study? What if I can disprove the medical profession and vindicate those whose suffering and anguish comes through with every word I read? Simply put, I want to prove that one can successfully ignore a limb that is not part of one's reality.

And yet, despite all that has happened today, this afternoon I feel better than most days, even my upsets feel different, lighter, and more transparent, less of being in a fog. And I realize that I have become quite comfortable walking with my arm in a sling and using my right side only. Is this what it would feel like to walk with only one arm, all the time?

CJ, from my favourite website, said that he bought a wheelchair and would drive to a different part of his city, where people didn't know him, take the chair out and wheel himself around. He wanted to see what it would be like not to have the use of his legs. He said that those days were the best for him, the only times that he felt complete, and that he felt perfect. He wrote that it was always with a sadness that he returned to his car and put the chair away. That's how he knew that his double-leg amputation was the right thing for him. He went to India for it. He is now very happy. Of course, that's not what I want. I don't need nor want surgery, I just want to prove that what these people are feeling is not psychological, but physical.

I turn east on Queen and walk slowly past rundown stores, second-hand furniture outlets, small art galleries and vintage clothing establishments. They have added a brand new, shiny Shoppers Drug Mart on the south side, incongruous to this area. I keep on walking since I don't know where I want to go. I reach the library and cross the street to the north side. I am undecided.

I need to call the school.

I don't want to.

How personal should the journal I am supposed to be writing be? Should I even bother with it? I should if I want to help others.

I contemplate going as far as the Gladstone to have a sandwich and a drink at the bar, but it's quite a walk. I go towards it anyway.

It *is* a long walk, past Jameson, past Lansdowne, past all the new hipsters' hangouts. There is even a new trendy brewery, serving home-made brew and pub fare. Walking is good and I feel better.

I step under the new bridge that reconnects Dufferin Street north and south of Queen Street. Its newness clashes with the area, but then so do the condos rising everywhere. Everything changes.

I stand in front of the Gladstone but don't go in.

I change my mind and turn back.

Lisa, with her very round head and all smiles and laughter, sucked me in. I am so naive. I misinterpreted the friendliness, the neighbour thing. As soon as I get home, I'll find the right home service to wash my arm, so that it doesn't become an impediment to the experiment.

I look into the tacky store displays. I am hungry, but I can't decide what I want to eat. I become quite indecisive when I'm upset. There are too many choices these days.

I need to get some painkillers, I can stop at the drug store for them.

There are no liquor stores in the area, a reminder of its dry days and I don't feel like going all the way to Liberty Village to get some Scotch.

I need to eat first. I walk in front of Danny's, a new sandwich takeout place that opened last fall and that has become one of my favourites. It is very clean and the servers wear those thin food handler's gloves every time they serve you. I respect their attitude towards germs.

I must admit that I miss my mother's home cooking. Maybe, if she hadn't kicked me out of the kitchen every time

I ventured there while she was preparing a meal, I would have learned to cook a good Irish meal. Now that she had passed away, I eat out all the time—mostly I go to places where I can trust the hygiene. I don't go to Irish pubs, maybe I should. Irish was not popular while my mother was alive. But now, it's all the rage, with new pubs opening everywhere.

My students won't miss me today, they like it when a teacher is away, gives them a bit of a holiday, especially if there is no work left behind.

I go into Danny's and I am the only customer at this time of the day.

Chicken breast, no cheese or onions on the sub. Everything else. Toasted. On whole wheat bread, of course. It's always the same.

"Thank you."

I must remember that mother had it hard, orphaned early and shipped to Canada when her aunt found out that she was pregnant, passed on from one family member to another, feeling unwanted, only nineteen. Aunt Emma was kind to her, looked after her and became her surrogate mother, and that was a blessing. Childless Aunt Emma was strict according to mom, but certainly not mean. Mother helped Aunt Emma run the boarding house and look after the lodgers. My birth in Toronto shortly after she arrived must also have been difficult for her. Understanding this did not make it any less painful for me, the recipient of all she had suffered, and was still suffering as I grew up.

I grab the sandwich and walk home. Being one-handed is becoming normal. I am thankful no one is out, and I don't have to see or talk to anyone on the street, even people that I just know by sight.

Mother was not one to speak harshly of Aunt Emma, first because as she would say, one should not speak ill of the dead, and secondly because of what Aunt did for her. Once though, when coming back from some errand that I don't remember, mom and I passed by St. Vincent de Paul Church on Roncesvalles.

"It's amazing, look at those columns, mam."

She didn't answer me. I stopped to take a closer look. She waited for me. The front looked like the entrance of Roman or Greek temples I had seen in history books.

"Such an interesting church, right, mam?"
"Stop annoying me, Jack."

I hadn't done anything.

"There is nothing amazing or interesting about this church, it's falling apart that's what it is. And to think that Auntie was going to give them her house in the will. Father Salamano, an awful waster, urging her to donate to the church after she died, because the church was falling apart, because the parish was poor, and they had no money, what malarkey. That old eejit *was listening to him, nodding her* ceann *like a donkey. Can't believe she thought about it…"*

I had never seen my mother go into such a rant, the more so one against her aunt that she adored. I later found out that every time mom contradicted her or did something wrong, Aunt Emma would say, "Lassie, mind your manners, I'll call Father Salamano right now, and sign away. You'll find yourself on the street." Mom imitated an old Irish woman's voice when she said that.

She rarely spoke that way about Aunt Emma, and as if to make up for it, for the next few weeks she also told me how kind and generous she was to us, that no one else would have done what Aunt Emma did, and how she would scratch the eyes out of anyone who said anything bad about her.

I am barely finished my sandwich and those fleeting recollections, when there is a knock at the door.

I seldom answer my door when I am home, a policy of mine. No one ever comes to visit me. Those that knock are always strangers that I don't want to see.

I clean up the little mess that I made while eating my sandwich. I wipe things more than once and always with a clean cloth. I have stacks of those cloths under the sink.

The thumping persists, unlike the knock of most salespeople or canvassers who after a while get discouraged and leave. Of course, some, like this one, are more tenacious than others. I just ignore it.

I sweep the dining room floor. I still eat in the dining room, and sit where I always sat when we lived with the lodgers. Even with my mother no longer here, I can't eat anywhere but in this room, it was the rule, never in my bedroom, not even in the kitchen. She had many rules and enforced them. If one wanted to eat supper at the Hughes house, lodgers and family alike, it had to be at seven on the dot. Lodgers who had shift work were lucky, she made exceptions for them. I am sure some lied about their shift work in order to get around her rigidity.

The knocking gets louder as I reluctantly make my way to the front door, ready to yell at some poor door-to-door salesperson, or worse, at some well-meaning Jehovah's Witness who does not know about canvassing etiquette.

I open the door and Lisa is standing on the other side of the screen.

The first thing that I notice is that she has buttoned up her blouse to the top.

Her face is red, and she looks determined. She speaks through the screen door as I fumble to get it open with my right hand.

"OK. I'll do it, in your kitchen. Right now, if you still want me to…"

She spits out the words very quickly as if afraid she will forget or regret them.

I am not sure this is what I want anymore. After I finished eating, I had decided to find a private home care service. I hesitate, still smarting from the earlier rejection. Not sure I can trust her.

"I am sorry, I was unkind earlier, Jack. You must admit your story was quite… unusual. But I thought about it, I see all kinds of things at the hospital. Nothing should surprise me. But I didn't expect it from a neighbour, especially you."

I was apprehensive, but the thought of a clean arm, and not having to wait a couple of days for a specialized service, was too tantalizing to give up. It will do in the interim.

"Thank you."

I start walking towards the kitchen with Lisa following me.

"Thomas called and said that there was an important meeting at the college. He had forgotten to tell me, he's going to be late…"

The way she said it, emotionless, unusually flat for someone so perky, made me wonder if there was more, but I didn't really care.

She mumbles to herself, "I don't like it when he works late. Too often…"

I don't know how to respond.

She cheers up.

"On the positive side, it gives me a chance to be a good neighbour. And Jack, *you* have a real problem."

She keeps up a nervous monologue, while I continue to say nothing. She walks behind me, talking to my back as we make our way to the kitchen. I don't want to chat about *my problem*, it is just about washing the arm, and I already regret saying yes.

"You must wonder why I changed my mind."

She grins.

"We all have our problems. I also don't have many friends; all my friends are really Thomas', he made sure. I understand your predicament…"

Not sure if she meant the lack of friends or the arm. At this point it does not matter, I just want to get it over with.

"Thank you for changing your mind."

"You don't have to thank me… I'll pretend that I am at the hospital. Anyway, he is making a habit of these late nights at work, and I don't like it, but who am I going to tell? So you see, you can be my sounding board. You tell me your problem and I'll tell you mine. Deal?"

She chortles, but it's not funny. I am not sure this is what I want, what I had anticipated.

I see her eyes wander all around, the door to my room is open and her gaze goes there. My room is always clean, so I don't have to worry and my bed is fully made. It's the first thing I do in the morning. She stops and looks into the dining room.

"Nice place. Spotless for a guy. I mean it's good. Nice to see."

"I just keep it clean. As I told you, I am not a big fan of dirt."

"It smells good too, you should come and do my house."

"I…"

"Just kidding."

She finally stops prying around, stares at me, making sure that I was serious and she wasn't an idiot for trusting a strange man, a next-door neighbour. Still looking in my eyes, she says, "I changed my mind because… because, well… there are other people like you. Not many but some. It's called BIID, Body Integrity Identity Disorder. I almost didn't believe you at first. But, it's a real medical condition, and I am sorry."

It was brave of her to come into a stranger's house and offer to do me a favour, I must admit she either has guts or is totally naive. She is wrong to assume that I didn't know about BIID, of course I have read about it, much more than she can imagine. I am committed to several Internet groups. It's not as black and white as one might think.

There are so many gut-wrenching stories.

ES recounted how he put his leg into a bucket of ice for six hours. How he went to Emergency and that they had to amputate his foot. How he is now happier than he has ever been. It led to a long discussion on the pros and cons of fooling the medical world. ES did remind us that the pain was excruciating and it wasn't for everyone.

TM said that he knew doctors in Mexico that would cut off a limb for $10,000 or $15,000 at the most, so that you didn't have to go through that whole pretending scenario. He knew people who had gone there and had an arm amputated. He said that it was quick, painless and that they finally felt normal. Members of the group, showing their prejudice, weren't sure they wanted to trust a foreign doctor, and others saw the cost as prohibitive. In general, people lamented the fact that no one in their own country understood.

I know their stories by heart and more, there is nothing new that she can tell me.

She has no clue about what I know, and what I have gone through.

"Thanks for doing this, Lisa, I appreciate it... BIID... it's complicated. If anything, I have a greater fear of microbes, which is why you are here. I'm just doing an experiment and I could handle it if I didn't feel the need to be germ-free more than other people."

"OK, you know better, although I still think you should see someone... whatever, let's get started."

I don't answer her, and leave her to think what she wants to think.

I am wearing an oversized, long-sleeved, V-neck polo shirt and nothing else underneath it. I am becoming quite good at choosing clothes that I can easily remove or put on. I am thinking about how I will look when I take my top off. This was beginning to feel real strange, and suddenly my anxieties kick in. Not knowing what to do, I don't move.

Without saying a word she grabs my arm, pulls my sleeve up and over my shoulder so that my armpit is exposed, and asks me if I have a clean washcloth. I point to the second drawer beside the dishwasher. I have dozens of clean ones. She opens it and pulls one out, puts it under some warm water and adds hand soap from the pump that is nestled on the ledge of the sink.

"I have had patients that had anorexia, I guess what you have is a bit like that."

She is insistent and I don't like it. Lisa gently squeezes the excess water from the soapy cloth and starts washing the arm. She goes up and down, applying pressure as she moves along, and it feels so good. I guess it is the massaging effect on an arm that had not been touched all day. It is worth every awkward moment I have spent talking to her, and I know I need to talk to her, if I want her to continue.

"No, I don't think it is… yes, I guess you can say that it has some, a few similarities. But it's different…"

"How… tell me more, I'm curious. It's about who you think you are, what you think you look like. It's about self-identity, right?"

I didn't really want to get into this. I knew this would happen. I knew she was going to go there and make me analyze it. I hate the word "self-identity," everyone uses it, mostly in the wrong way. These are battles that she knows nothing about. I sigh.

"Not really, I am not sure I want to talk about this, Lisa, all I can tell you is that there is no treatment for BIID."

"Now *that* I don't believe, remember you are talking to a nurse."

She takes my limp hand with her left hand and with her right hand begins to wash each finger, including the crevices between them and it feels incredible, even a bit sensual. She wraps the warm cloth around each finger.

"How do you like living here?" I ask.

"Changing the subject, I see."

I laugh.

"I am sorry, I don't like talking about my personal life."

She snickers.

"Well, you shouldn't have asked me to do a personal thing like washing your arm."

"I am sorry."

She goes back to the arm and scrubs as hard as she can, rinses the soapy water out of the cloth and starts again.

"OK Jack, you get to ask me a personal question, and I in turn get to ask you something."

I am not sure that is any better, I was expecting to not do any talking at all. I guess I can't have it both ways. I reluctantly play her game, but it has to be the first and last time.

"So you don't like when your husband works late?"

Might as well get personal, see how she likes it.

"It's not that, it's more that I have long shifts where we don't see each other, so you would think that the nights I am home he would make a greater effort not to work late. I understand, he can't help it, he can't time his work to my schedule, but it's annoying."

Her fingers are strong, reaching deep into the muscles. I nod in agreement.

"I can see how it would annoy you."

I suddenly and unexpectedly feel the coming of an erection as her bare hands caress the length of the arm. I feel it getting stronger, and need to stop it. She rinses out the washcloth one more time, and I pray that she doesn't notice the bulge I am hiding as I lean against the sink.

"My turn: have you ever told anyone else about this problem?"

Maybe if I tell her something serious, it will go away.

"Yes… well, I tried to tell my mother, when I was a kid."

I look at mother from the floor where I am sitting, leaning against the couch and reading. She is resting and watching TV. This is her break from the hard work, when she has her tea and a slice of warm apple cake—sometimes she puts a little bit of vanilla ice cream on top. She is a good baker. I can smell the cinnamon. I also get a slice, but I am too young to have a spot of tea, she gives me milk instead. I would love to go and snuggle against her, but I can't, something tells me that it is not right, and I don't know why. She seems not to like it when people get close to her, she tenses up.

I have the new Archie. I love my comic books, I have thousands— maybe not that many, but I have a lot. I like being in the same room when she watches her show at tea time. I look at her and she has her serious look, it makes her look angry, even when she is not. She doesn't lean over and touch me, pat me on the head or hug me, like we see the people in Weatherfield do. My mother does not like touching people either. That's okay, I am happy just reading and being in the same room.

She watches Coronation Street *at the same time each day. She stops everything when it is on. It starts when I get home from school. It is the only show that she never misses, she likes Mr. Fairclough. I like rubbing my right hand against the brown corduroy of the couch while I read silently. I use my right hand. My left hand wants no part of it. It doesn't like touching anything, just like my mother. Touching things revolts it and that's why I missed the ball last week and everyone laughed at me. Mother doesn't like me talking while she watches, but I am allowed to talk during the commercials.*

The Cheerios commercial comes on, it is my favourite cereal.

I cry out.

"Mam, there is something wrong with my left arm, it feels weird."

It just came out, I hadn't planned it.

"Nonsense, normal people don't have weird arms, Jack."

"It's different."

"What are you talking about? Is it longer, shorter than the other? Do you want me to measure it?"

Lisa grabs the dish towel that hangs near the stove, and dries my arm and then pulls the sleeve down.

Mother sounds annoyed.

"No, mam."

She briefly glances at it.

"Fatter, skinnier?"

"No, mam, just different… like it doesn't listen to me when I want to catch a ball…"

She has a strange look on her face, and says, "Jack, I am sure that the arm is fine, and even if it isn't, no one is perfect…"

I can tell that she doesn't believe the story about my arm and does not want to talk about it. I can tell I am annoying her. I try one more time.

"When I run, it doesn't move like the other… "
She is not listening to me, but continues.
"… and we can't all be athletes, teachers make good money, you should be a teacher… "
Her show starts again and she stops talking. I go back to reading.
"What a hussy, that Marjorie!"
Another commercial break.
"Of course, Jack, we can't always be perfect or get what we want, but we must try anyway… "

Lisa massages the dry arm one last time.

Mother says a few other things. It has nothing to do with my arm.
I am glad when the commercial ends and she goes back to watching Len Fairclough, who is just coming home from seeing Marjorie Proctor. By virtue of watching all the episodes with her, I know everyone in the show.
Maybe I didn't say it right.
When the show is over she turns to me.
"Jack, I can't believe it… I can't."
"My arm, mam?"
"My Lord… "
"What, mam?"
"Len just died."
I hadn't been paying attention and missed it.
She roughly grabs my arm and looks at it, compares it to the other. She frowns.
"Jack, there is nothing wrong with your arm, it's just you."

As soon as I am done telling this story to Lisa, I regret having said so much. It was a silly story, I can't blame my mother for everything.

"I am sorry, Jack. I wish she would have had more empathy, even if it was in your head."

Talking about my mother has done the trick. I'm no longer excited, my erection is gone.

"I am sorry if I bored you with my stupid story."

"No, not at all, I like listening to people. I like talking but I like listening as well, you learn so much."

She was a good listener, I must admit, very attentive, very encouraging with her eyes, the opposite of my mother.

"Thank you for listening, and for washing my arm."

I actually felt better having told her, although it did feel a bit like I was betraying her memory, a bit like I was "speaking ill of the dead." Nevertheless, it was cathartic.

"I hate to see people in need, it's my weakness. I am sorry, I sounded so mean earlier when you asked me to wash your arm."

"You weren't mean, I was just a stranger asking for a weird favour."

"Whatever it was, I am happy to help, we should talk more about this BIID. I am intrigued by it. Plus, I hate to admit it, but I have no one to talk to outside of work; people talk about friendly neighbourhoods, but people don't really like talking to their neighbours, they don't *really* want to befriend you."

I don't want to argue with her or start a discussion about people, I am one of those who do not want to befriend anyone. She starts walking towards the door and I follow her.

"Thanks, Lisa, thank you very much…"

"It was nothing. I'll come every couple of days to wash it, more often if I can."

We exchange phone numbers.

9.

I was happy that Lisa washed my arm yesterday; the arousal was a bit embarrassing but I managed to hide it from her, and it won't happen again. I am really not attracted to her, I think it was more about the massage and the fact that I had accidentally seen her naked breast earlier in the day while she was bending down. I am certain that it won't happen again. My taste in women, if you can call my limited experience that, is quite different. Marie and even Paula were tall brunettes, serious women.

I feel good this morning. I called in sick, explained that I hurt my arm, and will be in tomorrow. I apologized for yesterday, saying that I was at the hospital, after falling off a bike, and that my phone had died. Celeste, from the school, genuinely felt sorry for me and told me to get better. I wasn't happy at having lied to her, but I had no choice, and now, I have a whole day to myself.

I take a quick shower. Of course, not using the left arm slows me down, but I am a fast learner and I already find shortcuts. Not having to go to work, I decide to take my time, thinking mostly about how I will describe what I am doing, in my yet-to-be-named blog. I will start with my encounter with Lisa. I will change her name. I don't struggle as much with my clothes. Only using my right hand is already becoming routine.

I go for a walk on Queen Street but today I walk west, towards High Park. It is an unfamiliar feeling to be walking the streets and not have to go to work, but a good one. I don't think I have ever taken two days off in a row, and not really have been sick. The north side where the sun is shining feels wonderful. The neighbourhood is changing, hipsters are taking over, creating a make-over I am not sure I like. A few storefronts refuse to change, like the lady who makes those strange little bronze sculptures. There are a lot of vintage shops on this block that slopes towards the lake; it appears that a new one opens every day. I like looking in the windows but I would never buy my clothes second-hand. My mother would call the used shoes sold in those stores "dead man shoes."

Walking along, enjoying my morning smoke, something catches the corner of my eye, and forces me to stop. In the storefront window I see my pale reflection and a life-size male mannequin wearing a nineteen-fifties suit and a fedora. Chartreuse is one of the older vintage boutiques we have in the neighbourhood. They have an interesting window display every month, I look forward to them; this one was new to me.

The mannequin reminds me of someone I think about once in a while, someone who wore a similar suit when I was younger, when my mother was still alive. A man whose suit was way out of style in the early eighties when I first met him. At that time, people were wearing bell bottoms, colourful shirts and wide lapels, but not him, he looked like someone out of the fifties.

I light another cigarette out of habit, a filthy habit, really. Maybe it's time to quit, I had never thought of it or wanted to quit before. The smoking started as an act of rebellion against my mother. One of the few battles I had ever won with her, well, almost, I could smoke as long as I did it outside and away from the house. She let the lodgers smoke on the porch.

It is quite eerie seeing those clothes in the window, it brings back memories.

I remember running inside the house one day after having played soccer by myself in the alley. I was getting better and better at keeping the ball in the air, my record was twenty bounces using my feet, my head, my torso, and my knees before it hit the ground. I would run with the ball and kick it at a target I had drawn with red chalk against the side of the garage. The alley was often deserted after school and became my personal soccer field; it ran almost the whole length of the street, behind the houses. All the garages were in the back and accessible only by this alley. I was quite good at guiding the ball where I wanted it to go, to push the ball just ahead of me, without losing stride. It was all about the foot, right and left, and the ball. I didn't have to look at the target, striking the ball at the right place with the right part of my foot was the key, since I always knew where the target was. I practised over and over. Not having any friends had its benefits; no one saw my mistakes or made fun of me when I missed. I moved side to side dodging imaginary opposing players—stones I had placed in the middle of the alley—running around them, stopping abruptly and shooting. I made up different situations and never got tired of playing. Soccer was the only indulgence my mother allowed in my life, and I could hit the chalk-drawn target on the garage door as many times as I wanted, as long as it was between the time the lodgers had left for their evening shifts and the time the day crew arrived home.

That day, dripping with sweat, I ran straight into the kitchen to grab a snack. I could smell the stew cooking as soon as I got into the house. I liked the smell, but I didn't like the meat, whether it was beef, or lamb on special days, like St. Patrick's. I liked the big pieces of carrots and potatoes much more than the fatty meat. She only made that large pot of stew on Sundays, it was unusual to have it in the middle of the week, unless it was left over. The smell of cooking stew was a comfortable smell. She let it cook for a long time, often listening to The Dubliners or another record from Aunt Emma's collection of oldies.

Surprisingly, my mother was not in the kitchen. I see her sitting at the dining room table talking to a man who is standing and wearing an ill-fitting suit, from decades earlier, and also holding a fedora in his right hand. I realize that he is a potential lodger and the smell of a home-cooked meal is serving a dual purpose. To entice him to take the room and to feed the lodgers.

I had walked in on an interview, which my mother conducted with all potential lodgers. A room had become available; we had five that we rented out while we lived on the main floor. My mother had the front room as her bedroom and she had carved my space out of an oversized mudroom adjacent to the kitchen. The room was quite large and I was grateful to have my own bedroom after having shared hers for many years. The back room had a door to the backyard, which was useful for when I got older and started drinking.

My mother had a long set of rules which she divulged to potential lodgers only after she had assessed their moral fibre and their ability to pay room and board on a continuous basis. The important rules which she had them sign for were mostly about not smoking in the house, not cooking in the room, no noise past 10 p.m., and absolutely no women visitors in their quarters.

I am surprised we even had any tenants that still wanted room and board. In our area, boarding houses were all being replaced by rooming houses. A cheap hotel had even opened up, behind the old Greyhound terminal. We were a dying business, but maybe because we were the last one we still attracted some renters, mostly English, and a few Polish immigrants who wanted more than just a room, who wanted a bit of a family dynamic.

Mother had precise times for breakfast and supper. There were specific laundry days when she washed their clothes. She was strict, but the lodgers did not complain. They appreciated all that she did for them, she made them feel at home, acting as their surrogate mother, and she never knew how much her attention to them hurt me.

"Jack, say hello to Mr. Raymond Masson."

"Hi."

"And now, leave us be, please."

She doesn't have to say it twice. I don't like lodgers. This one looks different. Dressed like a gentleman, like one of those rich people you see on TV, but with old clothes, so old that even I can tell. Our lodgers work in factories, and some as far as the stockyards. Sometimes they smell bad when they come home from work.

I watch the two of them from the kitchen without making any noise. They soon forget about me.

"Mr. Masson, let's be honest shall we, I like you, but I am worried that in your condition you may be let go from your job, and will not have money for the rent."

She has not offered him a seat, or a glass of water, which means that they are not finished; she only does that after she accepts them as lodgers and they sit to sign the household rules as well as the rental agreement. And of course, pay first and last. Sometimes when things are slow, we accept weekly lodgers, but prefer monthly or yearly.

I wash my hands and get an apple, the only snack I am allowed before supper. I have to wash up before I grab any food, and I have to rinse the fruit because they are touched by everyone at the market and are full of germs according to my mother.

There is a long, silent pause as if the man is not sure as to what to say next.

"Mrs. Hughes, with all due respect, I believe that you run a fine house here, you have a good reputation, and I am happy to see that there is a strong sense of order, a good stew on the stove, and that there is no room for not knowing your rules, and I am ready to accept them. As for impugning that I may be a risk because of my disability, I will not accept that. I have worked my whole life as a printer. My accident came quite early in my career, and I have never missed a day's work. I was just transferred to Toronto from Montreal by my company. I will always pay the rent, on time; that is a guarantee. My references will speak for me, you may call my employer, or my union."

There was more silence. He is not disrespectful but there is something about how he talks. Something my mother would not want in a lodger. She likes it when they are a bit afraid of her. He obviously is not.

My mother keeps looking to the left side of this Mr. Masson, and then to his face. She always worries about trouble and is very mistrusting. The man turns silently and stares at her, and it is then that I notice what disability they had been talking about. I notice the empty sleeve; this Mr. Masson had only one arm. It is my first time seeing a man without an arm.

There is a long pause.

"I appreciate your words, Mr. Masson, and I believe you. Have a seat, would you like a glass of water or lemonade, tea per chance?"

"A glass of water would be very much appreciated, Mrs. Hughes."

He sits down very slowly, majestically, leans over, uses his sleeved stump to hold the paper down, and with his right hand signs the agreement.

"Thank you, Mrs. Hughes, I will be a good tenant. I will see you on Saturday."

I bring him a glass of water without being asked, and stay there.

"Thank you, son."

Saturday is moving day for our lodgers. They don't usually bring much with them.

After drinking quickly, he gets up, and as he walks by, the empty sleeve brushes against me. He goes through the door being held open by my mother, turns around and smiles.

I wash my hand as soon as I return home from my little jaunt on Queen Street. Mr. Masson was a nice man. I liked the way he spoke to my mother, he was not afraid of her, having one arm only made him stronger, far from being imperfect, as my mother thought he was.

I put the sandwich I had bought for lunch on the dining room table; this is the largest room in the house, with wide French doors to the hall and an entrance to the kitchen. It was also where the lodgers dined and relaxed. My mother had set up a couch and a TV in the corner. She also had a shelf for books and magazines they could borrow. The only phone on the first floor was here; the lodgers used the one on the upstairs landing. The lodgers played cards in the evening, never for money, at least not when mother was looking. Some played checkers, a few played chess.

I hadn't thought of Mr. Masson for a long time. He was an avid soccer fan and we listened to European games on Sunday, on the radio, while we sat on the couch and my mother cleaned the dishes from our lunch. I would help her for a bit and sit for a bit. He loved and knew everything about soccer. When he found out that I was also crazy about the game, he would tell me stories about the upcoming matches, analyze the results, tell me which teams were going to move up and which would be relegated. Marseille, in the French leagues, was his favourite team. He had worked in that city on the docks as a young man, before becoming a printer. He told me about Robert Schlienz, a German soccer player who lost an arm after a car accident but that it didn't stop him from continuing to play soccer. He mentioned that this one-armed soccer player became the captain of his team and led them to two national championships. Mr. Masson was also the only lodger that liked my mother's black pudding. She didn't make it too often, but when she did, he would always compliment her. I also used to like it, until I found out what it really was. As I grew older I gravitated towards the different potato dishes my mother made—she had hundreds of different ways of making potatoes, and I liked them all.

A couple of months after moving in, I overheard my mother and Mr. Masson speaking quietly on the couch while listening to the radio.

"Mrs. Hughes, pardon my indiscretion, but what happened to Mr. Hughes?"

"Mr. Masson, those are not questions one asks a respectable woman."

"I am sorry, Mrs. Hughes, I mean no disrespect. Young Jack was telling me that his father was dead but he didn't look sure. He seemed rather confused."

"And that is another thing, I would prefer you did not meddle in our personal affairs, Mr. Masson, I don't want you talking to Jack about those things. He is a sensitive lad."

"I agree the kid is a good boy, he just needs a father figure, or a bit more attention."

"What makes you think you know anything about chlann, children?"

"I know about loving. And about a father's presence in a boy's life."

"Blow not on dead embers, Mr. Masson. Do not speak about what you don't know."

"I will do as you say, but I will not be rude to the young lad, and I will answer the questions he asks. Goodnight, Mrs. Hughes."

"Remember, just don't be talking about things that are none of your business."

"I suppose I am still allowed to talk to him about soccer? And what about you, Mrs. Hughes?"

She mumbled something and I couldn't hear the rest. I was happy that he stood up to her. At the same time, I was surprised to see how curt she could be towards him. I thought she liked him. She looked at him and treated him differently than she did the other lodgers. Only later did I realize that on that night, she had spurned his subtle proposal to be in her life as more than a lodger. She would not allow herself to fall in love again.

10.

Lisa is true to her word. Around two o'clock I get a text message asking if now is a good time. I say yes, and add a smiley face. I don't text much, since I don't have anyone I need to communicate with. The text option came as part of the phone package and although I didn't need it, I kept it. All my students were texting and they joked in class that I was *so yesterday* with the new technology. They said that no one phoned anymore, they just messaged, and I believed them. They showed me how to get emojis on texts. They had no trouble learning that and more when it came to technology, but could they remember a few grammar rules? Even Lisa was comfortable texting. I am glad I kept the option.

The arm starts to hurt again. It only subsides after I take two extra-strength Advils. As the day progresses the pain gets worse. The arm needs to be massaged as well as washed, but I won't touch it. I will wait for Lisa.

Whenever I think of Mr. Masson I still feel guilty.

He had been a tenant for almost a year, and things were fairly cordial between my mother and him—she didn't trust him completely, but there was mutual respect and probably more. His one arm did not seem to bother her, it rattled her that he was not afraid of her, and although never rude, he always spoke his mind.

I often heard them discuss the "Troubles," while they sat on the porch drinking tea. At first I thought that the Troubles were about my mother's paranoia regarding the lodgers, but as they continued talking I learned that it was the Troubles between the Catholics and the Protestants. They both had their opinions and agreed to disagree. I didn't know my mother followed politics, nor that she could smile and blush when talking to a man.

Mom and Mr. Masson became friendlier, from time to time they watched television after the evening clean-up. The other lodgers were on the porch, joking and smoking, we could hear them; I was reading the latest Spiderman issue and they were sitting on the couch. I wasn't paying much attention to them until I heard.

"I am sorry, Mrs. Hughes, it must have been terrible."

Their voices suddenly turned serious, both stopped watching a TV program where an ocean liner was battling a fierce storm, and I couldn't help listening to them.

"It was, Mr. Masson, more than you can imagine, passage on a ship was cheaper and they were not a wealthy family, I didn't know anyone below deck, I was sick the whole trip."

"How did you cope?"

"People were kind... an elderly Irish couple, also from Cork, looked after me on the ship, and they made sure I got on the right train to Toronto."

"It was not right of your aunt to send a young girl, all by herself, she should have made better arrangements, what were they thinking?"

"They were ashamed, they were poor, I was a burden to them, but I tell you, I didn't want to leave, I cried, I had friends there, I didn't care if everyone in Cork knew. I would rather have faced their dirty looks than to have been sent away. Aunt Emma had done well for herself in Canada, it made sense, but I never forgave them for sending me away, I never spoke to my aunt in Ireland or her family again. I have never been that scared."

"I don't know what to say, Mrs. Hughes, except that I am sorry that you had to go through that, it wasn't right."

I glance over and see that Mr. Masson has put his hand on hers.

"Mam, were you really scared?"

She quickly removes her hand.

"Jack, what are you doing hiding there?"

They had forgotten about me.

"Reading."

"Well, you are not to be eavesdropping."

"I wasn't, mam."

"It's OK, Mrs. Hughes." And he winks at me.

I was happy that they were getting along again.

When mother was cleaning the rooms and I was home from school, she asked me to help her put fresh sheets on the beds. I followed her around because it was the only time I was allowed in the lodgers' rooms, and because there was no saying no to my mother. Although I didn't like the lodgers I was curious about them. Their rooms were mysteries, each one was different. The furnishings were varied, but the differences were in other things as well. Each room had a disparate aura, a unique smell. Some rooms were quite spartan; others had sentimental knick-knacks on shelves and dressers. Some rooms were messy; others were very organized. I found it interesting that a room that had been extremely well-kept by one lodger would morph into a messy room when a new lodger took it over. The room took on the personality of the person living in it.

I helped as best as I could. I would straighten one side of the bed and then mother would come over and do a perfect nun's cap. She was a perfectionist about everything, whether making the bed, washing dishes or cooking the perfect meal. I stopped following her around when I was twelve; at that point I was more interested in playing soccer outside than seeing the inside of the lodgers' rooms. The rooms no longer held any mystery for me. I had a narrower view of life: everything was about sports.

But there was one chamber that I was still curious about and when my mother asked me to help her bring the clean linens to that room, I jumped at the prospect. I had stayed home from school because the night before I had felt sick, but now I was fully recuperated, and bored. It was raining outside. I had always wanted to see Mr. Masson's. I had wanted to see how different the room of a one-armed man was from the others, and this was my opportunity.

I follow my mother in, and the first thing I notice is how neat the room is. Everything is in its place, just the way mother likes it.

"Jack, this is what a room should look like."

The second thing is the smell; a man's scent, strong, different but not unpleasant. It is a nice change from the other lodger's rooms where, until my mother opens the windows, the stench of dirty sweat bowls you over.

"Jack, you see, a man does not have to be a pig or live in a pig sty."

The third thing that I notice is that there are books, a lot of them, and of all sizes. I guess it has to do with the fact that he is a printer. There are oversized hardcover books with pictures, some smaller hardcover books, and a lot of paperbacks.

"Mr. Masson reads a lot," my mother says when she sees me looking at the books.

"You should be doing more reading yourself, instead of always playing soccer," she adds.

"I will try, mam."

On the night table beside his bed is a big book with a black jacket cover. There is a picture on the front cover. It's a photograph of a sculpture of a naked man and a naked woman holding each other and about to kiss, their lips almost touching. It feels wrong staring at that image. My mother has not noticed me looking at the book. I move and stand between her and the night table. The title of the book is The Sculpture of Auguste Rodin.

I stare at the cover—the kiss I don't care for, but the sculpture shows the woman's naked breasts and legs, and she is not wearing any underwear. My mother still has not seen what I am looking at, but yells at me "to get moving." She throws me a rag and tells me to start dusting, and stop staring in the air. I dust the night table, and while polishing the top of the table, and making sure that she can't see me, I open the book. There are more photographs of naked people in it. The page that I had just opened the book to shows a woman with arms around her head and also totally nude, with her body coming out of a rock. I close the book right away.

I dust the wooden front of the armoire.

The image of her breasts, and the area between her legs, stays with me while I continue my chores. My mother is finished with the other side of the bed and makes her way where I had been standing. I move towards the bookshelf and turn my back to her.

After a while she tells me to grab the dirty sheets and pillowcases and leave them in the hall on top of the others.

When I come back, I see that she has turned the book over, and that on its back there are no pictures or words, just a shiny black cover. We move on to the next room, but all I can think of is about what other pictures may be inside that book.

The rest of that day I was obsessed with Mr. Masson's book. I didn't know anything about sculptors or sculptures and I didn't know that you could show nude pictures in books. I began hatching a plan to see that book again.

It wouldn't be too difficult—my mother had duplicate keys of every room. She kept them hidden in the back of one of the kitchen cupboards. She was very discreet and made sure no one was in the kitchen when she accessed them. I had seen her take them and put them back many times.

It is so hard to wait, once I have decided what to do. I am very excited. As soon as Coronation Street *comes on, I make my way to the kitchen, prop a chair against the counter and very quietly, from the very back, slowly open the cookie jar where she keeps all the keys and take out Number Three.*

I am lucky that all the lodgers have day shifts this week and that there is no one in the house except for me and my mother.

"What are you doing?" Mother yells from the dining room where she is watching the opening credits.

I turn the tap on. "Getting a glass of water, mam."

"Going to my room to read," I add, hoping she wouldn't question me. She doesn't.

I know she will be occupied for the next while, she never leaves the room when her show is on.

I slam the door to my room, without going in, and quietly creep up the stairs.

I sneak into Mr. Masson's room and the book is still there on the night table; my mother had left it face down, she didn't usually move things belonging to the lodgers, but here she made an exception. She must have been upset at seeing that picture, and I must remember to put the book back the same way. I am so nervous—I have never done anything this bad.

I grab the book. It is heavier than I imagined. I close the door and go into the lodger's bathroom, which I am not allowed to use, turn the light on and sit on the toilet.

There is a knock on the door and I know it is Lisa and this time I am not going to make her wait. I smile as I let her in.

"Hi Jack, how is the arm?"

"Hello neighbour, in need of a good washing. I took a shower this morning but ignored it and I am not sure if it's in my head but it feels pretty grimy."

"Probably mostly in your head, but it is what it is, let's get to it. You are lucky that these are my days off." She winks at me, and I don't dislike it.

It feels rather good to have such a familiarity, which surprises me. It is not something I would have thought I would have liked. I had been warned so many times by my mother not to get too familiar with any of the lodgers; she barely tolerated that Mr. Masson befriended me and talked to me about soccer.

It is amazing how fast things become routine. I follow *her* to the kitchen this time.

"How was your morning, Jack?

"Great, I went for a walk and never felt better."

She rolls up my loose sweatshirt all the way to my shoulder, gets the clean sponge from the counter. I had switched to a sponge and left it ready for her. She wets and soaps it.

"Jack, I have been doing more research about BIID…"

"Please, Lisa, let's not spoil the day. I don't want to talk about it, and I'll tell you honestly, I have probably read more than you will ever read on the topic."

"That may be so, but all the doctors that I know routinely tell their patients not to engage in self-diagnosis…"

I interrupt her, without trying to sound mean.

"But, I should let *you* diagnose me, right." I grin to let her know that I still appreciate what she is doing.

"Well yes, you should. You say you don't want to see a therapist or go see a doctor, so I am your next best thing."

"That's if I wanted to talk about it, which I don't."

"Well, we have to, if you want me to continue washing your arm, which is a pretty big favour I am doing you. Look, we can continue our little game, you answer one of my questions and I will answer one of yours. Any topic, within reason."

She washes the arm with the soapy sponge and it feels so good, just like before. The massaging of the arm that I had held so stiffly during the night and this morning is way too enjoyable. She has such strong hands for a small person. I should have paid for professional massages long before this.

"You can start, Jack, ask me something."

"What's your favourite colour?"

"You're being silly… fine, yellow. What's yours?"

"That makes sense, you are a bright, shiny person… mine? Blue. Good, we are done."

"Come on, Jack, be serious; ask me something else."

I need to think of something that will make her not want to play this game anymore but still wash the arm. I know she wants to get to my issues and I don't want to go there. Let's see how she likes it.

"OK. What is the biggest problem between you and your partner *right now*, the one that makes you feel awful, the one that's a deal breaker, if it doesn't get resolved?"

"Well done, you went right for the heart. Let's see… "

"If you are going to think about it, it can't be the biggest issue."

"No, I'm just trying to find the right words… OK, here goes nothing…"

She takes a deep breath.

"I want children and Thomas doesn't… I'm not getting any younger and neither is he, and I don't know how we are going to resolve this without one of us getting hurt, or having to give in."

I don't expect people to be that honest. I should have known. Lisa is different. She is not playing games with me. Her answer throws me for a loop.

"Wow, that's a big one."

Fortunately, and maybe fearing that she had said too much, she quickly jumps to another question for me.

"My turn. Are you attracted to amputees, to women who have missing limbs, like in a sexual way?"

I also didn't see that one coming, but I realize as she says it that she *has* been reading about BIID. Probably had gone to some of the sites I had been on. That theory had been debunked many years ago. It was more like a sexual fetish by a few. Not at all what I felt, or how anyone I knew felt. It actually trivialized the problem. It generated quite a few on-line discussions.

I laugh.

"You are way off base, Lisa. I am attracted to women that have *all* their limbs, in fact, tall brunettes are my kind," I throw in to bug her. "Seriously, I don't have a fetish. I hope you read more than that—that's such an old theory, a bit insulting, really."

"Sorry. So, and be honest, OK, was there a relative, a neighbour, anyone in your life that was disabled, missing a limb?"

"No."

I didn't want her to play amateur psychologist.

I know what she is trying to do. She read how people with BIID may be psychologically affected by events in their past. I know I should tell her about Mr. Masson, about the sculptures but she would misinterpret that, and jump to a number of simplified and mistaken conclusions.

"I know you are trying to figure me out. There is nothing to figure out. Listen, it is very simple. The whole medical world, well, those in it who are interested in this issue, have a hard time figuring out the people who suffer from BIID. Experts believe that the feelings BIID people have are illogical desires, that they have this desire to have their body physically match the image of it that they have in their heads. It's not that at all with me. I don't have a fucking, sorry, *freakin'*, idealized image of myself, I don't see myself with one arm, all I have, all I know, is that this left arm does not belong to the rest of my body, there is a toxicity in it that I need to deal with. The argument that all these too-well educated doctors are tiptoeing around is the possibility that we may be hard-wired to not recognize part of our body, and if our brain does not think that it is there, then it is not. They know that this possibility exists, because doctors have seen it in stroke victims. Part of their brains shut down. The section that recognizes that one has limbs stops working; sometimes that issue can be fixed when that part of the brain is restored, sometimes it can't. But what if you are born that way and it can't be fixed? What if you are born hard-wired to only have one arm, why would one deny people what they are born with? Look, Lisa, these people aren't crazy. I understand them. There are a lot of new studies that show that it may not be as far-fetched as you would think. I have folders and folders of information on it. But, having said that, *mine* is a different battle. I am ignoring my arm, as one would ignore certain things in their lives that pain them. I am also trying an experiment. It's personal."

I hadn't meant to tell her all that, to give her a mini-lecture, but I was hoping to stop her inquiries to make her see that I knew what I was talking about, so that she could leave me alone.

"Sorry, Jack, I don't know what to say."

"It's OK, I have never had to explain this before. Look, it's like in the early stages of sex reassignment surgery—experts thought that any doctor doing that surgery was in cahoots with the patient's mental disorder and was colluding with them, instead of curing their patients. That these 'renegade' doctors were feeding their patients' delusions was often the accusation. You don't hear about that anymore. That's what people with BIID suffer, and I have to defend them."

"You make a good point, Jack."

She stops talking, and becomes reflective.

"OK, Jack. I enjoyed our talk, I've got to go now. I'll see you tomorrow."

She looks defeated as I walk her to the door. I hold out my right hand.

"Thank you, Lisa."

I open the door and feeling sorry for her, I divulge.

"You are not completely wrong. There was a lodger, named Mr. Masson, and he had one arm…"

She lightens up.

And there in the hall, near the door, I tell her about Mr. Masson, and the Rodin sculptures, but not about my arousal when looking at them, just that I liked them.

When I am done, she seems happier. "Thank you for being honest, you're OK."

She leaves and I watch her walk to her house.

I didn't tell her what happened to Mr. Masson. I still feel guilty about it.

Of course, I wanted to see that book over and over. I had become obsessed with those images, almost as much as keeping germs off my body.

It surprises me that it was that easy to do and that I didn't get caught. Hidden in the washroom I am both excited and scared, shaking a little bit as I open the book. I see the pictures and read the names of the sculptures, written under each photo. I like Eve on the Rock, *even though she hides her breasts, like she was shy. She lets me see the area between her legs and that is what I stare at for a long time. I am curious to see what women have down there. It's like the lady in the sculpture is saying don't look at me but also look at me.* Awakening *is the one that I first saw when I opened the book. I flip to that area of the book and find it. I like this one a lot too, not more than* Eve, *but differently, I like that she does not hide her breasts and that I can also see between her legs, they both look the same in that area, very smooth. In the one called* Eternal Springtime, *it looks like it is the same woman, but now she is in the arms of a man. I can still see everything, and I especially like the way she shows the side of her chest. There are many others that I like, mostly of women coming out of stone and showing me their private parts. I quickly flip through the pages, each minute that passes scares me, I don't know how long I have been in the bathroom, and as I am about to close the book, I find a section on drawings and paintings. One picture makes me blush right away, and although afraid at being caught, I have to look at it a bit longer. It is called* Nude Woman on her Back. *I have never seen a drawing like that, it is even smuttier than the others. You can't see her face and there are scratches or lines all over the body, but she has her legs wide open and that very naughty part stares at me, and it's not smooth, it has hair, lots of it. Sitting on the toilet I can feel my penis twitching. I quickly close the book, and bring it back to the room, lock the door and make my way downstairs.*

"Just getting another glass of water," I shout, although no one had asked, and I quietly put back the key.

I had had erections in the past, but usually in bed as I woke up in the morning. I didn't know why or when I would get one, I didn't know that it could happen just by looking at something, just by looking at pictures. That was the first time and it felt unusual and strange in a good way. Although afraid at being caught, I knew that I had to see that picture again.

I wait a whole week before I try once more. I come home quickly from school and go to my room to do homework. As soon as Coronation Street *starts, I sneak out of my room, get the key and go into Room Three. The book is not on the night table but I easily find it on the bookshelf and take it with me to the bathroom. I skip the sculptures and go straight for the watercolours. There are other lewd drawings, more women with their legs open, more hair, more folds. I find the picture that I want and have been thinking about all day. This time I am expecting my penis to do something and it does and I enjoy it.*

I became braver and took chances by sneaking the book into my own room.

There, I sat in my bed looking at all the pictures, full of excitement, knowing that it was forbidden and that I was being mischievous. It felt good to be bad. To know my mother would kill me if she found out.

They were quite strange sculptures and paintings, some ugly and some beautiful, all by Rodin. Some of them were men and women without any arms or legs. Twisted bodies. But I only got excited when seeing women in all their nudity and sensual poses, which is what turned me on, not the number of limbs.

It has been a month, and I have memorized all the pictures in the book. There have to be other books that I can look at. I get the key, like I always do the moment I hear the music of mom's show. I know that from that point on, I can do anything I want to do. Mother will not hear me. I get another art book from the shelf, but before I take it downstairs, I linger in the room. I open the closet. There are very few signs that a one armed-man lives here. A few shirts have the left sleeve sewn, but for the most part everything is normal.

I close the door and make my way downstairs, thinking about Mr. Masson, distracted.

"What's that, Jack?"

Mother is standing against the double doors of the dining room. I freeze.

"What were you doing upstairs… were you stealing… what's that?"

I am in shock. Can't speak.

"Let me see!"

She grabs the book out of my hand, and looks at it.

"Mam…"

She slaps me, an open hand to the face. And it hurts.

"You little thief… meirleach… dirty little boy."

She slaps me one more time, with the back of her hand, and I start to cry as I run towards the front door.

"Get back here. Go to your room and don't come out until I call you."

I have never seen her so angry.

I go to my room full of shame, my head hurts and my red cheek is on fire.

JOHN CALABRO

Except for her proverbs, she never spoke Gaelic unless she was really mad or wanted to insult someone. From my room I listened to the activities going on outside of the door. I knew the routines of the house by heart. I was sorry that I had disappointed her. I swore I would never look at dirty pictures again.

Everything was quiet at supper. The other lodgers must have sensed that my mother was in a bad mood. They kept quiet. There was none of the usual banter about work, jokes about their bosses and their co-workers. After they had finished their meals my mother brought me a sandwich and I was to eat it in my room.

Later that night, I heard my mother and Mr. Masson talking in the living room. I stood against the door of my room to better listen.

"Mr. Masson, I apologize for my son's delinquency, and for stealing your book. He had no right being in your room. He broke the rules and he will be punished for it. No more soccer for him. He dishonours my house and my guests."

She can't do that, she can't take soccer away from me. I will run away.

"Mrs. Hughes, you are being too harsh on the lad. I gave him permission to go to my room anytime, to pick and read any of my books. I am sorry, but they were only sculptures, art by masters no less. There was nothing wrong."

He is lying to defend me and I like that.

"YOU, YOU gave him permission, and who gave you the right to give my son anything, any permission? Especially with the type of books that you have in your room. I will disagree, it is not art, it is filth, nothing but bruscar, *just garbage. This is my house. You are passing through, a vagrant of some sort, passing through, I tell you. YOU, you can decide what is best for my son? NO, you don't. You don't come into my home and tell me how to be a* máthair.*"*

She is scaring me, she is mixing everything up. I have never heard her fight with a lodger before.

84

"I will have to say, Mrs. Hughes, that you are too harsh on the boy. You are handicapping him; let the lad be, let him be normal. Boys are boys."

I don't know exactly what he means but I like that he is defending me.

"Mr. Masson, consider this your notice. You are to leave at the end of the month."

And that was it, they stop talking and I could hear him make his way upstairs, dragging his feet.

I didn't have the courage to say anything. My mother knew that Mr. Masson lied to defend me, and maybe because of that, she was so mean to him.

Mr. Masson left without an argument, and I never saw him again. He disappointed me, he could have bested my mother, he could have fought for me, for his right to stay. He left me a new soccer ball as a present, little consolation. And like my father before him, my mother never mentioned Mr. Masson again.

Maybe to make up for what she had done, after a couple of weeks, she allowed me to play soccer again.

I never forgave my mother for throwing him out and for slapping me. I continued to obey her, but something had changed in the way I saw her. I still wanted her approval, but she wasn't perfect anymore. It didn't matter what the lodgers said. She wasn't the saint they made her out to be.

11.

For a long while, I felt guilty that because of me my mother had thrown out Mr. Masson. Much later, as an adult, I realized that there was more at play, mother was afraid of Mr. Masson, fearing mostly of falling in love with him. She was afraid of getting close to a man, any men, afraid to leave her shadows behind. Unfortunately, I couldn't help her.

I hear my phone's text messaging alert.

In one hour?

OK, I text back.

I have not called the school since I told them that I would probably be in the next day. I am not sure why I am being so stubborn about giving them an explanation, an indication of my plans. I get phone calls from people whose numbers I don't recognize and I don't answer. I have a lot of messages. I listen to them but don't reply. They are mostly people I don't want to talk to, my union rep at school, my curriculum leader, twice, Celeste, three times, and the supply teacher they have hired. My other colleagues won't notice my absence, unless I have become a topic of gossip. My students are the only ones affected by my disappearance and knowing them, they will have fun making life miserable for the supply teacher. I need a break from school, and don't feel like speaking to any of them. I force myself to stay in bed past what is usually comfortable for me. My back is sore from staying in bed too long; the arm, stiff, to my side, is also in pain. I am a mess this morning.

I force myself out of bed.

I shower and that, at least, is much easier. Every other part of my body co-operates to speed up the routine and avoid the left arm. Knowing that Lisa will wash the arm today also helps. My right arm is in charge while I get clean. I leave the left one to dangle uselessly. Nevertheless the whole morning process is tiring and time-consuming. Today I feel irritated, contradictory and impatient. Revisiting the Mr. Masson episode was unpleasant, it brought back some of the confusion about my mother. I want to forgive her, but even after all these years, I'm still trying to figure it out. The arm always hurts. I doubt myself, I doubt the whole value of this exercise. I go from elation to depression too quickly, too often during the same day. I am not sure what to do next, I thought that I could just go about my days in a normal way except that I wouldn't use the left arm. It sounded so simple. I should have known better.

Something about yesterday left me with a bad taste. Too much analysis from Lisa, too much talking by me. Maybe I should have been more sympathetic to *her* issues, but I didn't want to get embroiled with something I knew nothing about. That's partly why I don't like talking to people, don't like making friends, it gets complicated very quickly, people misinterpret, people get offended. Being alone is much better.

With a towel wrapped around my body, I open the kitchen window and smoke a cigarette, standing there, leaning out, and making sure that I blow the smoke outside. I have never smoked inside the house, except this way, even after mother's death. A leftover from my mother's anti-smoking rules. She knew that I smoked and drank but never said much about it as long as I followed the same rules that she had for the lodgers. Marie didn't mind that I smoked but also insisted that it not be in the house, on the porch was fine, and I had to suck on a mint before getting close to her, a small price to pay. I still pop a tic-tac in my mouth after each smoke. It might have worked out with Marie if she hadn't insisted on my seeing a therapist.

My arm is not getting used to being ignored. It rebels by creating excruciating pain. Pain that I might be able to handle with the help of sedatives and alcohol, but I am trying not to give in. I have stopped drinking since I started this thing, and I want to take these extra-strength Advil sparingly, I want to feel the pain of the whole process. As if it gives it greater honesty.

I slowly and methodically put some clothes on—underwear, sweater and jeans, the minimal. Using only one hand forces me to do things differently, to think differently. I use my knees, my mouth, my feet, my shoulders, more efficiently. I am beginning to feel comfortable without the use of the left arm, which is also what this experiment is all about. I open the window facing the garage and the alley, have another cigarette, and a tic-tac. I am looking forward to having Lisa work on the arm, it has become more about the massaging than the hygiene. I am not looking forward to her trying to analyze me.

Impatient and in need of a distraction, I go and tidy the kitchen, although I have not used it much. I sanitize the bathroom. I love the smell of a sterile space, which is mostly the scent of cleansing chemicals, of antiseptics. I like everything in its own place and disinfected. Cleaning with one hand is arduous and time-consuming, but satisfying. In a strange way, doing things with one arm gives me a sense of independence, and that makes me feel better.

There is a knock at the door.

Lisa is there.

She is smiling, and looks cute in tight black skirt and a thin white T-shirt that shows the outline of a red bra. She looks sweet as she smiles, very warm, very innocent.

"I cut across the grass, I hope no one saw me. The neighbours are going to think that I am having an affair with you." And she giggles.

She is right, the neighbours, her husband, society, no one would understand, they would misinterpret our relationship. It would be worse for her, she is taking a chance.

"If this is not good, I could hire a nurse. I checked a few home services for people who are sick and can't leave their house. You could help me find someone trustworthy."

"Except that you are not sick."

"I'm not?"

She winks.

"No, you are not, but never mind."

She seems comfortable with taking the chance, and right now I need her help.

"Do you mind if I smoke?"

"It's bad for you, you should quit, but it's your house."

I light up, and for the first time in my life, I have a cigarette in the middle of the house and not at the window. I blow smoke away from Lisa and into the hall. We have no ashtrays in the house, and so I take a decorative plate from mother's precious Royal Doulton collection and use it for my ashes.

"You are using *that* as an ashtray?"

I shrug my shoulders, take a strong, deep drag, and hold it in until my lungs burn, and only then do I let it out slowly. I take another puff and feel more at ease. I also cough.

"Smoking is bad for you, see, I told you."

I stub out the cigarette, only half smoked. I pop a tic-tac in my mouth and offer her one.

"Thanks," she says, and takes a couple. "You can take your sweater off if it makes you feel more comfortable."

She helps me take it off, and I notice how much easier it is with someone's help. Lisa takes the bar of soap in her hand, waits for the water to be the right temperature, tests it with her fingers, soaps both her hands and then uses those sudsy hands to slather the arm. This time, although both are available, she is not using the sponge or a cloth, only her bare hands. Surprisingly, she starts with a gentle touch, almost floating over the skin, spreading the foam the length of the arm.

I try not to move or say anything while the cramping subsides.

She softly brushes the palm of her hand against the arm, drawing circles and smoothing them out. Her face has a serious professional look, that infectious smile is gone for the moment. She adds more soap to her hands. Lost in her own world, looking down at the arm, she meticulously covers the underneath of the arm with the lather, and continues massaging upwards, finding different pressure points and then sliding downwards. She grabs the left hand and foams each finger, like she has done in the past, individually making sure that each crevice is thoroughly cleaned.

"I have to ask. What was your relationship with the person renting a room from your mother, the one with one arm, did you want to be like him? Did he ever touch you inappropriately?"

She says this without looking at me, still watching her own fingers as they slowly move up the arm, crossing seamlessly the invisible line between what is mine and what is not, all the way to the shoulder, massaging as she goes along.

"We are not going to start that again."

She stops and lets go of the arm.

"We are, if you want me to continue this. I am trying to understand you, it's why I am doing this… and by the way, you weren't very understanding yesterday. I told you a big, personal problem that was bothering me and you didn't react, didn't even ask me how I felt. You didn't care, it was obvious. That's pretty selfish, Jack. All you can think about is your arm. It's not just about taking, you have to give when you are with people."

"I am sorry, Lisa, but you were the one who changed the subject pretty quickly and also I am new at this sharing… "

"You make too much of a big deal. Just say what you are thinking, ask questions, and show that you are interested about the other person—it's in the voice, the tone, the eyes. Anyway, it *is* a bad situation, Thomas and I love each other, but how can we have a life together without one of us having to compromise? There is no middle ground, and it scares me."

"My mother had a saying for that, 'It's difficult to choose between two blind goats.'"

"That's a funny saying, not sure what it means but sounds about right, I have two blind goats, I lose either way."

"Sometimes she used two blind dogs."

She smiles and starts again, absent-mindedly, as she simply re-spreads the same suds, up and down the arm.

"What if you forced the issue, and got pregnant anyway, see what he does when really confronted… he wouldn't just leave you."

"That's a bad idea, I couldn't do that to him."

I don't know what else to tell her, I am not good with giving advice; growing up, my mother's idea of advice was repeating her favourite sayings and clichés, and she had one for every occasion. If she was here, she would say, "The well-fed person doesn't understand the hungry one." She was right,

I don't think people can truly understand each other and what they are going through, one can only be sympathetic and it wouldn't hurt for me to practice that a bit more.

"I know how you feel, Lisa. It is exactly the same for people who suffer BIID. There is no middle ground. If you go along with what society thinks you should do, you will suffer the rest of your life. If you do something about it that goes against society's definition of normal, you will be seen as a freak, as a leper, as a deranged person. But, I'm sorry, this is about you. What are you thinking of doing?"

She stops.

"I don't know, I hope that he will change his mind. I pick my moments to talk to him about it, to make him see how I feel. Except that when I do speak to him about it, he then avoids me and stays late at work. He also tells me that I am blackmailing him, that he is too set in his ways, that he is too old... he is only eight years older than me, I don't know. I'll figure it out. It's depressing me."

She starts again. The sparse, black hairs of my left underarm mix with the whiteness of the suds. Using her small, thin but strong fingers, she tugs at the edges of the armpit, gently pulls the skin back and forth until her hand stops and rests for a moment in the hollow of the armpit.

"So, you are not envious of people who are handicapped, you don't want to be like them?"

"No, not really, I liked Mr. Masson, but I wasn't envious."

"Why do you say that therapy doesn't work?"

"Of all the people that I know who post, every one of them has seen a psychiatrist and they all say that it did not do them any good. There are no drugs for it, and the suffering is so real, that the medical world does not know how to cope with it. Sure, we all get depressed because of it, and that's the only thing that they can do, prescribe anti-depressants so that we don't commit suicide. But how does it solve our problem? The only sensible stuff comes from a few researchers, outside the profession. And these people agree, that if there is significant suffering because of the disorder, then we are not choosing to become disabled, we already are. I can show you the studies."

As I am speaking, she continues and I don't know what to say or how to react to this tingling, intoxicating sensation of having her bare hands massage the arm. I also realize that I have just put myself into the same category as those who I have always described with BIID. I used "we." Although I feel different from them, I have just admitted to Lisa and to myself that I have the same symptoms.

Her wet and soapy fingers caress the protruding elbow of the arm. She bends the elbow and cleanses the bony part with her hand, turns the arm over and continues with her palm to prod upward using the back of her hand, pressing with her knuckles on the return journey. These up and down strokes give me goosebumps.

"Tell me more."

"There is nothing much more to say."

Suddenly, I am thinking about something other than those studies. Standing beside her, half naked, the back of her neck close to my lips, the way she is touching me, again I get aroused.

I try to ignore it.

She grabs a clean washcloth, wets it, and begins the task of scrubbing the affected arm. She still hasn't looked at me, her eyes follow the wet rag. It's as if I am not even there. She washes off the soap from the cloth. There is so much soap on my arm that she has to rinse it several times. She does not seem to mind and neither do I.

"What did your mom die of, if you don't mind me asking?"

My arm is fully sterilized. She is done.

"Cancer? It was in the bone by the time they caught it."

She twists the cloth so as to squeeze out every drop.

As if the last few minutes had only been a rehearsal, and when I think that she is finished, she applies more soap directly to the washcloth and starts again. It is as if she has forgotten what she just did. She drapes the wet cloth around the arm, rubbing up and down, encircling the arm, tightening, loosening, kneading, massaging as she re-washes an already clean arm. Holding my hand, she turns the arm over and washes the underneath with her other hand.

"There, you ask me something now."

She puts down the washcloth and uses her bare hands. She encircles the wrist with both hands and gently squeezes the excess soap, pulling at each finger, lingering in the fissures between them.

She is arousing me.

"How long are you going to wait until you make a decision, Lisa... you know, you are a bit like me. I was happy to just wait, not to do anything, feeling ashamed and hoping that one day it would go away. Are you hoping that your problem will go away, that Thomas, one day, out of the blue, will announce that he wants children? Because I don't think that's going to happen."

I might have crossed a line but I am also getting excited, and I can't have her stop now. I need to keep her talking.

She doesn't answer but doesn't stop either.

"I don't know..."

I start imagining that she might also be getting excited, but she is so deep in thought, I don't think she is even noticing.

I am hard and brushing gently against her side as much as I can without being too obvious. She must be feeling my hardness against her leg. I'm more stimulated than I have ever been. Different than when I was with Marie. I don't want this feeling to end.

"You are right, and maybe I am deluding myself."

She gently brings the arm under the faucet to rinse it out. She squeezes the arm downward, directing the dripping water into the sink.

She stops, and there is a moment of complete silence except for the sound of the water flowing noisily into the sink. I am as hard as I can be. She lets my arm fall gently to the side of the sink, grabs the dry towel, turns off the faucet, and begins drying the arm. She drapes the towel around it.

I am not sure how long I can contain myself, before she notices it. I turn a bit to the side, leaning slightly against her as I pretend to rest near the counter.

She focuses on drying the arm. She holds it with one hand and dries with the other. She rubs from the wrist up to the bicep and back to the wrist. She lets go of my hand and using the towel, she strokes up and down. I close my eyes. I am almost there and I rub a bit more against the side of her naked leg.

"Is this arousing you?" she suddenly asks.

"No…" I stammer, caught by surprise, and she knows that I am lying.

She ignores what I said and continues stroking up and down. I am confused, still stiff as I can be, ready to explode, I am not sure if I can hold it, nor do I know how to answer her.

"Jack, I want you to be honest with me… is this arousing you?"

"Yes…" My cheeks are on fire.

I expect her to drop my arm, to leave me stranded and to run out of the house. Instead she continues and lets me sway against her.

"It's OK. Sometimes my patients get aroused when I give them a sponge bath, they can't help it…"

As she leans towards the sink to put the towel down, the side of her breast inadvertently brushes against the naked clean arm. I close my eyes and explode with such fury that I am forced to bend over the sink and to hold on to the ledge with my right hand. I suppress my heavy breathing, but shake as I keep ejaculating. I open my eyes. Lisa is watching me, but to my surprise she is not repulsed. She has a smile instead.

"But I must tell you, Jack, not speaking strictly as a professional but also as your friend, I have to say that you being excited…"

She looks down to where I am still hard and where there might be a wet spot.

"Shows me that your little experiment is doomed to fail. I may be delusional, you may be right about a lot of things, but to be honest, I am not sure I believe what you are saying about your arm…"

"What are you talking about?"

What is left of my erection goes down.

"You are right, Jack, you have problems, but…"

"You don't know what you are talking about, Lisa."

I lose my erection completely.

"OK, if that's how you want to play it, Jack. But is it not true that every time I wash your arm you get sexually aroused?"

I am starting to hate her.

"Your arm is quite normal, like everyone else's."

"What?"

She grins as if she caught me.

"My dear Jack, if your left arm can get you that agitated, and you were plenty agitated, I could see it and feel it, then that arm belongs to you, it is part of you, it is normal…"

She hands me the towel, gives me a peck on the cheek and goes towards the front door. There she turns to face me.

"We all have our problems. You will have to find how to deal with yours, but it's not in your arm. I'll see you tomorrow. Don't worry, I'll keep washing your arm, until you figure it out," she says with a smile.

I don't move from where she left me, and I don't answer her as she walks away and says, "Trust me, the arm is yours."

12.

"Trust me, the arm is yours." The words, and her victorious, self-righteous voice keep repeating in my head. I haven't slept very well the last couple of days, only in short fits, since that afternoon. Entrapment is the word I would use. I know she thinks she is helping. She is wrong. She had no right to test me, to set a trap. It is no excuse. What she did was not fair.

My cellphone rings. I'm not answering. Let the school figure it out. I am using my sick days, and I am not talking to anyone. Let them think what they will. Let them fire me. They can believe that I am very sick or that I quit. I don't care anymore. Even Lisa had the audacity to text me yesterday. I ignored her too.

I can't believe her—all sweet, all lollipop, sunflowers, geeky, awkward self, and then she pulls a stunt like that. Sexual entrapment, she should work for the vice squad. At least Marie never tried to trick me.

"Trust me, the arm is yours."

"You have problems... "

She doesn't know anything. Suddenly she is an expert. How is she resolving *her* problem? She didn't look too smug when talking about her precious Thomas and his fucking issues.

It's not her, it's the arm. The arm just played her. Like it has played me for a long time.

The arm, the arm, the arm, always the arm.

My blood boils, my right hand closes into a fist, my breathing gets heavier, my mouth clenches tight as a swelling rage grips me.

"Trust me, the arm is yours."

Fuck you.

Her words make me furious and I try to temper the mood. I lie back and light a cigarette. My first time ever smoking in bed, that's progress. I smoke in the house now, although, I don't enjoy these cigarettes as much as I used to. I use an empty water glass as an ashtray, take deep breaths and calm down. Smoking still serves its purpose.

Lisa may not be completely wrong. The experiment could be the problem. Trying to ignore the arm because it is not mine sounds juvenile, quite stupid really, of course, no matter how much I ignore that limb, it is still attached to me. I can't ignore the blood vessels, the nerves, the muscles or anything that connects the arm to my shoulder and to my brain. How silly of me. She was right without knowing it.

I know where I went wrong. I was trying to disprove some idiot who said, "… If it really stemmed from the brain, there would be symptoms beyond just the desire to amputate; it would be difficult to use the limb, or there would be signs of neglect on the limb." I wanted to prove that one could force the brain to create this neglect, but in reality I was looking for half solutions.

Mother used to say, "If it's drowning you're after, don't torment yourself with shallow water," in that thick accent of hers that I often found embarrassing in public and that I now miss. I never thought that I would find myself agreeing with one of those cliché sayings she was continuously spewing.

Lisa was right, I was trying to fool myself, to get away with something I shouldn't.

The arm wants to be a part of me so that it can continue to make my life miserable. It is plain to see now. The other day was a perfect example, even as I was having a most pleasurable moment, just like when I was with Paula, the arm made sure it turned ugly.

I stewed all day yesterday over that comment, *"Trust me, the arm is yours,"* which kept repeating in my head along with the image of Lisa's sad-sacked face. I stayed in bed, did not eat, nor shower. Probably the first time in my life that I skipped my morning shower. I did take a quick one before going to bed… habits. The only pleasure I took was in ignoring first her texts, and then her call to come over and wash my arm. I don't need her services anymore.

Today is better, and I am seeing things for what they are.

"Trust me, the arm is yours."

Fine!

My mother said the same thing thirty years earlier. Big deal. OK then, if it's mine, let's play.

I smash the usually limp arm against the wall to my left, as hard as I can. I am using it, see, there, that will make everyone happy. *Smash.* Yes, I am directing it, *content, Ms. Lisa.* I slap the wall with it. It hurts. It feels and it conveys the pain to my brain. That should make Lisa and the rest of *normal* society exultant. I smash it again. Ouch! What? Not as enjoyable as when Lisa was massaging it, right? Proves the same point, doesn't it.

I stop for a moment. I have just destroyed the experiment.

I don't care. If anything, it fuels my anger. What an ignorant *experiment.*

I hit the wall with the back side of the left hand even harder. At least the cramping is gone.

"Trust me, the arm is yours."

And so it is. I start again pounding the wall until I make a hole and pieces of plaster fall on the bed.

I hit everything I can reach, the wall, the night table, the bed, the headboard. The arm does not stop me, now it listens to me, *now.* The knuckles get the brunt of the hits and they burst in agony. I break the skin against the wall and the pain gets worse.

I see blood running down the arm, but it only encourages me. Using my right hand, I smear the blood, oozing from broken skin flaps, all over the left arm, *there, happy*, the arm that everyone believes is mine. What gives them the right?

Never mind Lisa and her help, her talking, her asking questions, her analysis, her trying to make me see I was a *normal* human being. I don't need a neighbour's help anymore. Never did, why did I even start?

The arm had betrayed the spirit of the experiment, mocked me all this time while I thought it hung there uselessly limp. It had used Lisa against me. It had used sexuality against me. Fine, thank you. Never again. The blood on my knuckles drips on the bed and I wipe it on the sheets. I am confused, happy, excited and I also cringe at the mess I am making.

I light another cigarette. It feels good. I blow circles and calm down.

Never again will I allow people, past or present, or the arm to hurt me. I'll do the hurting and the leading from now on.

The pockmarked wall behind me is smeared with streaks of blood and the bruising on the left hand is starting to show splotches of brown that I know will turn into black and blue welts. It will be a good reminder.

"Trust me, the arm is yours."

It has a new meaning now. Cigarette dangling from the corner of my mouth, finally exhausted, I fall backward on my bed and grind my teeth.

The phone alerts me of an incoming text and I read:

5 minutes? Can we talk? Are you upset? You didn't answer my knock yesterday. You are upset.

I don't answer her message.

The hand with the frayed skin around the knuckles further dirties the sheets while I move around.

Lisa is right. The left arm, the hand, they are both attached to my body. They are connected to my brain and my mind can't disconnect them. But, it does not mean that the arm belongs to me, it does not, it is toxic, always has been, and I don't want it anymore. Just because it is attached, it does not mean anything. Just because a sixth toe is attached, it does not mean it has a right to be there, that it should be there. My experiment was ill-conceived, I realize that now, but the reason for it is still valid. Whether I was born with this imperfection or I or my mother created it, it doesn't matter.

I guess I should be thankful to Lisa, she helped me see something that should have been obvious.

I light another cigarette, get up and take inventory of what there is on the first floor.

No sooner do I get up when there is the expected knock at the door. She thinks that she has me all figured out—so I got excited, it has nothing to do with the arm, if she really knew men, she would know that getting aroused does not mean anything more than what it is. She may even flatter herself that I was attracted to her, I was not, I am not.

I don't answer the door. There is no way she is touching the arm or me again. I let her knock, until she stops and I hear her leave.

Almost immediately there is a text on my phone. Just question marks, no words.

Ignoring it, I continue with a more important task, which is to make a note of what is in every room and to choose the right furniture or appliance.

The knuckles have stopped bleeding and are beginning to scab.

I start with my room, a double bed, one night table with a lamp and an alarm clock radio. There is a tall, five-drawer dresser, which might do the trick except that there is not enough space for it to fall cleanly.

My phone, still on the kitchen table, rings. I let it go to voice mail.

A closet for my clothes, a chair, and a small, wooden bookshelf full of heavy books, but the issue is the same as the dresser; the bed is in the way.

People should never test anyone without telling them. She shouldn't have done it, even if she was right. I hope she realized that now. I wish her luck and hope she resolves the issue with her husband, but she should leave me out of it. She is also right about me being selfish.

She had an answer for everything. When I told her about my high school date with Paula as another example of how my left arm betrayed me, she didn't see anything odd about it, she said it was typical of a teenager to be nervous at that age, especially around girls they liked.

"When you are an anxious person like you, it is very likely that your body would react strangely," she said. "Whether you like it or not, you are normal, a bit odd, but normal, maybe without knowing it, you are trying very hard to be abnormal."

I didn't need her cheap analysis, especially since she is way off.

The same with dropping the ball as a child—it was her contention that I had blown up the incident way out of proportion, that it was typical for kids to be uncoordinated. I had told her too much.

I resume my tour of the house and look into the kitchen. I let the left arm swing freely. I don't want it to cramp up, it's not important anymore, except for smashing it against the wall, I don't feel like using it for anything else. Maybe the stove or the fridge. The fridge is a possibility but probably too awkward and too heavy. I could pull it forward. I will keep the fridge in mind as a last resort. A small breakfast table, cupboards over the sink, one free-standing hutch that holds plates, glasses, and cups, and that is also a possibility. I can already see the mess. I cringe at the scene of broken dishes flying all over the kitchen. There is also the dining room, adjoining the kitchen.

My cellphone rings. I don't recognize the number. I listen to the message.

It's Lisa—from her landline, I would guess.

"I know you are home... Jack, I am sorry I hurt your feelings, it wasn't my intent... I'll come and wash your arm and won't say a word about it... promise... I was wrong to push you... Jack... I need to talk to you. I'll come by later, please let me in then."

I don't call back.

I go to the dining room. Designed to host our lodgers' meal time, a long, heavy table made of dark wood, seating eight, centres the room; four sturdy wooden chairs on each side were plenty, since we never had more than five lodgers. I now use that table to do my marking. There are always two never-ending piles, one for marked papers and one for those to be marked. If I ever quit teaching, I won't miss that. A china cabinet for the better dishes and glasses and a liquor cabinet are against the wall. There is nothing else in that room that I could use, maybe the TV near the couch if it had been the heavy old one, but I don't think this thin HD TV will work. I go through the double doors that give into the hall.

There is no use going upstairs since all the rooms there are now empty of furniture. I gave away or threw out everything that was upstairs when my mother passed away, right after I got rid of the last lodger. I was going to make the second floor my apartment and leave the third floor empty, but I couldn't, those two floors were always for the lodgers.

From the hall I move into my mother's room. This room I had left untouched for five years. Marie thought that it was morbid to do that, and along with my issues and my anxieties, it added to the shopping list of what made me, in the end, a less than desirable partner. I go in that room once a week, on Saturdays or Sundays, and open the windows to air it out. I dust and vacuum, and then leave the room as is.

Today, I open wide the windows that give into the porch and then go and get a new pack of large, green garbage bags from the kitchen cupboard. I decide not to involve the left arm in this affair. I find the sling and hastily shove the arm in it. I shake and open wide the bag.

With my right hand, I dive into the top drawer of the long dresser where she kept her clothes, grab as much as I can hold and shove it all into the garbage bag. When the drawer is empty, I move to the next one and slowly, mechanically, fill the garbage bag with her socks, underwear, blouses, bras, nylons, sweaters, pyjamas—anything I find. I shake open another bag and throw in all the trinkets that are on top of the dresser. Mostly Irish-themed worthless knickknacks, souvenirs from Cork that Aunt Emma had left behind. The silver shamrock earrings I keep. Mother was not stylish, but when she thought she needed to impress, like when we went to the bank to see the assistant manager, or to the lawyer, she would put on the shamrock earrings. To look nice, to bring us luck, but also just in case they were Oirish themselves and might be inclined to give us a better deal. They were her prized possession, and I shove them in my pocket. I go to the closet, and there her dresses, pants and drab blouses are still hanging where she left them. I unhook the hangers from the bar and throw the lot into the same bag. The same thing with her shoes, boots and slippers. I continue at a steady pace to get rid of everything that belongs to her. I don't want to stop and think about what I am doing. I have now filled three of those large bags. I go to the bed and remove the cover, the sheets and the pillowcases, and those I also throw into another bag; I decide to get rid of the pillows as well so there is only the bare mattress and box spring left, those will go out on garbage day. This is something I should have done years ago. I take the full garbage bags one at a time to the basement door, tie the tops using my mouth and one hand, and then with a swift kick I send each bag tumbling down the stairs. Five bags, five trips, five kicks, and I am done.

I go to the kitchen, change my mind. Turn around and go down the stairs to the basement. I place the bags neatly against the unfinished wall, and find the large box that I am looking for. Among the assorted tools that I have never used and various cans of screws, nails, washers and metallic pieces that I don't recognize is a thick rope. I take it with me and as I glance at the bags full of my mother's stuff, I feel a twinge of guilt at never having been able to mourn her properly. Until now, I have never known how to deal with my feelings towards her. Very early, at about the time I realized that my arm was acting up, I had trouble dealing with the idea that in many ways I both liked and didn't like my mother.

Back in mother's room, with the windows wide open, there is an appreciated cool breeze coming in and I unravel the rope. Mother used it as an outdoor laundry line, attached from the outside of my bedroom to the garage. When she did laundry for the lodgers, she hung their clothes there to dry, to the consternation of our neighbours who thought it an eyesore. I cut the line down when the last lodger left.

It wasn't that mom was a bad woman. I came to the conclusion that she just didn't know how to raise a child she wasn't sure she wanted. Maybe I reminded her of my father.

The only thing left untouched in mother's bedroom is an old, and very heavy, four-drawer wooden filing cabinet where she kept all the financial records for our boarding house. She even kept the old financial records of Aunt Emma's. It was full to the brim. Our home was a business and she treated it as such. She did not believe in throwing anything out and kept meticulous records, for her own personal satisfaction and for income tax purposes. She always gave receipts and declared all income and expenses from renting the rooms. She kept everything in that cabinet. I decide not to empty it until it serves its purpose.

I need something else from the basement, and go back.

In one corner, there is a pile of bricks that my mother used to create shelves for the lodgers; she would set two columns of four bricks by four bricks and place a wooden board on them, add another set of bricks on the same corners and place on them another board, and in this way she created shelves of various sizes that could accommodate the whims of different lodgers. I take two bricks with my right hand and bring them to mother's room, and make the trip three times. I make a row of two bricks high along the same wall that the filing cabinet is located. The cabinet is situated between the end of her bed and her dresser, and if it were to fall, it would miss both and crash on the carpet, in the space between them. The only problem is that the drawers will go flying open and hit the bed, dispersing everything in them. It won't do. I go back to the basement, find a grey duct tape roll and I use it to seal all the drawers tight.

I stand to the side of the cabinet, put my foot against the bottom, and use my right hand to pull the cabinet towards me. It will not budge. I try again, and nothing. By rocking it and adding more force, I finally get the filing cabinet to tilt a bit and I am able to hold it in an angle against my body. I slowly let it lean into me a bit more.

I count to three, jump out of the way, and let the filing cabinet crash to the carpet. It falls on its side exactly where I expect it to fall, and to my pleasant surprise the duct-taped drawers stay shut.

I try lifting the cabinet up with my one hand, but I can't, it's too heavy.

I quickly un-tape the drawers, ripping energetically, and remove all the file folders full of papers, and then I take out the empty drawers.

I now need to work quickly, time is of the essence. I lay three bricks against the wall where the bottom of the filing cabinet was resting. I add a second layer of bricks on top of the first three.

I can easily lift the frame back up and I am able to set it on an angle, resting on the bricks. It stays put. I replace the drawers, throw in the files. I keep checking the balance so that it stays up while still leaning away from the wall. I almost feel guiltier at having messed up her accounting and filing system than I do at having unceremoniously gotten rid of her personal belongings and thrown them into the basement. I re-tape the drawers shut. Everything is back to the way it was, except that the filing cabinet's bottom has one side resting on that row of bricks.

There is a large imprint of the filing cabinet left on the carpet, which I also need.

I tie the rope around the top drawer, looping it into the drawer's handle to keep it from slipping down.

The cabinet is now precariously perched on those two rows of bricks, leaning over but not falling. I go to the front door and unlock it. I kick open the door going into the hall. The drapes are pushed to the side. Everything is ready.

Anyone standing on the porch and knocking on the door can see right into the bedroom. I am surprised we were never burglarized. Maybe because my mother seldom left the house, and there were always people in the house moving about.

I take a deep breath. Everything is in place and I wait.

I take my arm out of its sling.

The text I have been waiting for finally comes through.

I am on my way to work, I'll come by in 5 minutes, please let me in.

OK.

☺

I lie down on the floor, put my left arm behind my head, across the recent imprint made on the carpet and wait until I hear her knock.

"Come in," I yell.

"One…" I take a deep breath, "two…" another breath, "and three…"

I pull on the rope, gently at first but without much success. I keep pulling with my right hand while keeping my left arm across the line and then I see the filing cabinet beginning to tilt, I brace myself, my body tightens, I grit my teeth, close my eyes. There is a delay and I open my eyes to see why, while pulling harder.

Something moves, life slows down for a breathless split second and then suddenly speeds up as I watch the filing cabinet come crushing down. I gasp, something cracks, pain shoots through the arm, my body convulses and I scream in agony.

My arm is pinned under an unbearable brutal weight and I can't move it.

13.

The taxi lets me out outside the wide entrance doors, under the bright orange signs. The garden centre to the right of the entrance is now open, a testament that the commercialization of spring is in full swing. The area has changed so much—I remember it as the real stockyards, that strange, smelly part of town where my mother would sometime come and purchase meat at wholesale prices. I would have to hold my nose, it was that bad. She would buy meat for the month and freeze it. From where I am standing, and if I think hard, I can see the cows go through long wooden corridors to an entrance leading to a building where only much later did I learn led to the abattoir. Sometimes, not sure how, a few cows escaped and then everyone gave chase. Often the police were called to help. Watching the news report about the escaped animals was always funny, I cheered for them but they were inevitably caught. Canada Packers took the whole north block and they made most of the smell. The pigs were slaughtered near the CNE grounds. I would see them with their snouts sticking out from between the planks, in those long transport trucks that drove east on the Gardiner below our neighbourhood. There was also a place up here where you could buy chickens at a good price, and mother would load up on them. She bought pieces of lamb for when she made her special stew. We took the Keele bus and I was there to help her carry the groceries. There are still a few meat processing plants left but for the most part, the factories and the smell are gone to accommodate the new houses mushrooming into neighbourhoods.

I should be feeling worse but I am not. Of course, the arm hurts, my pride is in shambles.

"What kind of stupid stunt were you trying to pull?" was all Lisa said on our way to the hospital. I didn't answer her. She drove me to St. Joseph, although it is close by and I could have walked. I was in pain and in no shape to argue with her. I was thankful she hadn't called an ambulance and created a spectacle.

I wondered how many bones I had mangled and if it was enough for them to amputate.

I look around me—they are building a new commercial centre and calling it The Stockyards where Canada Packers used to be. My mother would never recognize this area with its neat rows of carbon-copy houses, and the box stores that, like barnacles, attach themselves to these planned communities. They are all here: Staples, McDonald's, Starbucks, Canadian Tire, Futureshop, Rona's, Rexall, Metro and Home Depot, the store in front of which I am now standing.

The taxi drives away and the automatic doors open to welcome me.

The last thing I remember is seeing Lisa standing over me, and then I must have fainted. I later felt a wet cloth on my face, and then saw her efforts to lift the cabinet just enough for me to remove the arm. The pain was unbearable, but I kept my mouth shut. People say that mental pain is the worst, and I have shared that anguish, but physical pain is not any better. I barely got the arm out when she let go of the cabinet and it fell with a thump.

The neon-orange letters brag that the store is now open 24 hours; good to know.

I am a lot angrier that all my planning went for nothing, embarrassed that I had passed out, humiliated that I had allowed Lisa to see me in that state of weakness, ashamed that she had to help me crawl from under the filing cabinet, that I allowed her to drive me, and that I let her speak for me once at the hospital. She knew the people staffing the emergency ward, "He's my neighbour... he had an accident." She went about getting ready for work, and about an hour later, they took me into the back. The doctor said, "You are lucky, a clean break." And all I was left with was rage, that for all my troubles I ended up with a simple broken arm and a lousy sprained wrist. What a joke. They put a cast on the arm, up to my elbow and around the wrist, exposing fingers and bruised knuckles. Lisa came back to see me, looking very professional in her nurse uniform, almost sexy. She apologized for being unable to stay because her shift had started and after making sure that I had money for a cab home, she gave me a pitiful look and walked away. It was the look of "this man has crossed a line. He is not normal." That is how I knew society would see me, she was just like everyone else.

Inside Home Depot, arm in a brand new cast and in a clean, hospital-issued sling, it does not take me long to find the right aisle. Once in front of them, I did not expect such variety. I stare at the display. The arm is itchy and I can't scratch it. I could try inserting something like a screw driver, they have thousands here. The itching subsides as I twist the arm. I did not expect the arm to still be there, and now I don't know what rules regarding the arm I am supposed to follow.

These tools all look the same to me. I can see that some are aimed at the amateur and some at the professional. I contemplate asking someone but decide against it. All the information that I need is on the box and on conveniently placed information cards above each display area.

Lisa was furious with me all the way to the hospital. I am not sure what exactly she was angry at, maybe that I had spoiled her little plan to help me, to save me. Usually talkative she forced herself not to say anything except to give me nasty looks and mutter from time to time, "I can't believe you." Thankfully, it was a short ride, albeit unpleasant, made worse by my trying to hide the acute pain from her.

I could have gone to the hospital on my own. She had insisted. She has to stop helping me and I have to stop accepting her help, it's beyond being neighbourly, it's pathological. I can't help her with her issues and she can't help me with mine, the most I might do is to listen to what bothered her, and I was not very good at that. People would lead you to believe that listening could be enough, I don't think so, it never ends there. She can't know how I feel every day, and I can't know what it is like to want a child and the partner who you love does not want one. We are the only ones who can decide what's best for each one of us, to make our own choices and accept the consequences.

I decide to go with the Echo. Interestingly, all of them are painted bright red or shiny black, blood and death, I guess, as if there were no other colours in the rainbow. The real difference from what I can tell is that some are gas-powered and others are electric. I read the back of the boxes. The benefit of the gas-powered one is that it is cordless and more robust.

Thinking back, I can really be stupid. In the emergency ward, in more pain than I had ever felt, I kept hoping that the doctors would say that the arm was so badly damaged that they would have to amputate and that thought kept me going, allowing me to bear the hurt and Lisa's dirty looks.

I grab a display model.

I read that the gas-powered one can be heavy and noisy but provides unlimited mobility.

"No, thanks."

I reject the assistance from a man in an orange vest, wearing the corporate logo. I don't want him to start asking embarrassing questions.

I am upset at myself. What a stupid image it must have been, me pinned to the floor, a wooden cabinet trapping my arm and then to make matters worse, me screaming in pain like a bloody idiot, and then, to boot, fainting. What a childish "look at me" dramatic gesture, how contrived and dishonest. It will never happen again.

I pick up the electric one, ideal for light-to-medium tasks, perfect for "trimming garden trees and shrubs."

While in the Emergency, I remembered an article I had read, not totally related to my problems, but somehow significant as far as I was concerned. I had read about a family in Brazil, where everyone, all the children, were born with six fingers. They were all happy with this defect, loved each other, and lived a quasi-normal isolated life. One of the siblings was more sensitive to the bullying at school, and after years of public taunting, he cut off the extra finger when he became a teenager. Later, when interviewed, he said that he was happy to finally be normal and that no one made fun of him anymore and that it was an incredible relief. He said that the only regret he had was that his family no longer spoke to him, that they felt betrayed and that it saddened him to be left out, to have become an outsider to them. The story had little to do with my current situation but his plight resonated. It was mostly about his courage to do what he felt necessary, and the price he paid for it.

I take the box with the picture of the electric Echo and throw it into a cart.

I pay for it, and the lady at the cash, seeing the arm in the cast, is overly helpful. She double bags it and creates makeshift handles. I am surprised at how light it is, expected heavier. Not that it matters since I'll be taking a taxi back home.

The Internet has an answer for every question one might have about anything, and will even provide you with the perfect shopping list for any of your needs, no matter how morbid. I take advantage of that and get all I need at the Rexall pharmacy.

The bags are getting heavier but I don't have far to go. Across the parking lot there is a Metro, my last stop.

Once inside, I put the two packages in a shopping cart and look around for the meat department, which is not an easy feat in this cavernous grocery store. I finally spot the right section. A large man with a bloodied apron stands behind the counter, slicing thick steaks that he meticulously places on a tray. I am quite disgusted at the sight. I have not eaten red meat since my mother passed away. The butcher sees me, puts the flat container in the display rack, and comes over.

"What can I do you for?"

"Looking for about eight inches of beef shank bone… for my dog…"

The butcher smiles.

"Let me see what I have, how many do you want?"

I say two. He goes to the back and after a short while he returns with the desired pieces of bone, with bits of meat still dangling from them.

"That's perfect."

14.

Lisa is sitting on the steps of her house. She should be at work. I timed it so that she would not be around, that she would be in the middle of her afternoon shift. I am not sure what she is doing here. She gets up as soon as she spots me getting out of the taxi. The driver helps me. She watches me struggle with all my bags as I carry all three in my right hand yet does not offer to help. But, she does follow me the short distance to my front door.

"That was a stupid stunt yesterday, what were you thinking… and…" I tune her out. I am done with Lisa, with her neighbourly friendship, with her stroking of the arm, with her entrapment, with her help that goes too far and nowhere, with her being disappointed in me.

I keep walking. She must have called in sick, taken a day off, still worried about me. I have nothing to say to her.

"We need to talk… can I come in?" she asks, as I am opening the door.

I don't answer, but don't stop her and she follows me in. I put the bags down in the hall and it is only then that she realizes what is in one of the bags. She sees the picture on the box.

She grabs me by the cast and turns me around.

"Stop walking, let's talk. I thought that we were friends, or at least becoming friends. You need help. Let me help you. I talked to someone at the hospital, I can help you. He can help you."

"Do you want to sign my cast? I am sure I have a marker in the kitchen. That would be a great help."

I break away from her hold and go to the kitchen carrying the Metro bag. Using my teeth I unwrap the wax paper.

"What's that?"

"Beef shank bones," I say, enunciating every word separately for effect. I show her then re-wrap the package and put it in the fridge.

"Shank bones?"

"I like the marrow, it can be quite exquisite if you fry it the right way, and technically it's not meat. Bones are also great in soups, my mother made great dishes with them, this will be in her honour."

I want her to go away.

"Go ahead, sign my cast, you spent so much time washing my arm—write something nice since you two got along so well, and then you can leave, seeing that I don't need it to be washed any longer, since we don't need to be friends or even neighbourly anymore."

She looks at me incredulously.

"You don't make sense. What are you trying to do, Jack?"

"Nothing, go away and leave me alone, please. Pretend we never met. It was a mistake to start a conversation with you, no offense."

She stays, stands in the doorway of the kitchen, mulls over the insult. She suddenly jumps forward and shakes me by the shoulders.

"*What* are you going to do, are you crazy?"

"No, I am not. That's the problem."

My voice is matter-of-fact. I don't need her scolding, her analysis—I need someone to assist me, to help me. Period. I also know that she can't and won't and therefore she has to leave. It's that simple.

"Lisa, go home, please."

She stands a few feet away, with her round head and uncombed blonde hair all over the place, looking at me in a strange way, as if she wants to understand but can't.

I see her eyes get wet and a few tears stream down her face. She quickly wipes them away and I feel for her. She is really trying, and genuinely cares. But I can't let her manipulate me. I need to stay strong.

"Go away and leave me alone. Deal with your own problems. Find a way to have your child. Keep me out of it."

She comes over and slaps me with such force that I am pushed against the wall. It hurts more because I didn't see it coming. I rub my cheek. It smarts.

"You are an idiot," she says as she turns around and walks towards the front door.

I put the newly bought box on the dining room table, and try to open it with one hand, but it slips. Could they have made it more difficult? I put the box down and hold it against the leg of the table with a knee and try to rip off the cardboard lid with my right hand. The long staples are in too deep, machine packaged, they have it over my one weak hand.

"You are so stupid, and so selfish. All you can do is obsess about your arm. You are the most selfish man I have ever met."

I hadn't heard her come back into the kitchen and she startles me.

"You can't even open the box and you want to use a chainsaw…" She spits the words out as she shakes her head.

"Thank you for your opinion, Lisa." With as much sarcasm as I can muster.

She grabs the carton with her two hands, and with a fury I had not seen in the little time that I had known her, she rips the lid off the box and throws it across the room. She tears some more cardboard and drops it on the floor. She manages to destroy the package to bits while littering as much as she can. She then tears the chainsaw out of the plastic bag it came in and turns the plastic into a ball and flings it into the dining room. She is creating a mess, knowing quite well that the disorder will upset me as much as her anger.

She grabs the chainsaw, and brings it to my face, blade inches from my eyes.

"See, it's real. It's not a game."

She grabs my right hand and pushes it against the chain. It hurts. She presses harder and I get a small cut on my finger.

"Ouch, what the feck—"

"See, blood, see, it cuts, see, it hurts."

I take my hand away, and put the finger with the small cut to my mouth to stop the bleeding.

Who is crazy now?

"Thank you. You have been a great help. You have to go."

"Do you even know how to operate it?"

"I'll learn. Leave."

She won't. We look at each other in a type of stalemate. Her anger and her inability to protect me in some strange way makes her vulnerable and almost prettier, but it's never been about that.

"I am not crazy, Lisa. There is no cure, there are no drugs, I told you, and you know it..."

I am suddenly very tired of arguing with her. I stop talking.

Lisa comes forward and puts her arms around me, but I stand straight, rigid, and I am unresponsive to her hug. I don't want her to convince me not to go through with it. I won't let her manipulate me again. She pulls me tighter and I feel the crush of her breasts against my chest. I gently pull away.

"Jack, Thomas is coming home soon. Promise me you won't do anything crazy tonight. At least wait until tomorrow. One more day, please, one day won't make a difference. Please."

I need her to leave me alone, to stop wanting to help me.

"When did you get your tattoo?"

"What?"

What was she really about? Why did she care what happened to me, she just couldn't be such a nice person? And if she is, it has to stop.

"The tattoo on your chest, did you get it before or after you met Thomas?"

"What does it matter?"

"Nothing. Show me your tattoo."

I don't know why I am even asking. I have this idea, that maybe it will make her leave me alone, maybe she'll think that I am a pervert and go away forever.

"What?"

"..."

She is not saying anything, I don't think she knew I had noticed it or cared, since I had not mentioned it before.

"Why, that is stupid."

"A trade-off. Show it to me and I won't do anything tonight."

"No."

"OK then, goodbye, Lisa."

The way I say it, she knows she no longer has a hold on me, she has no cards to play, and has to leave.

"You promise?"

She is bluffing.

"Yes!"

She stares at me.

"No, I can't… " and turns around to leave.

It worked. She is not the only one who can play games, who can manipulate.

She suddenly turns around, plants herself in front of me and lifts her top, exposing her tattoo, mostly hidden by a shiny blue bra, and looks me in the eyes.

I hold her stare.

"I can't see the whole tattoo. Show me the whole thing."

I am pushing it, but that is the only way to get rid of her. I brace myself for the slap or an outburst as one hand lets go of her top.

"Jack, that's not… "

I keep staring at her.

She hesitates and then lifts her bra above her breasts and I see her full tattoo. It is a small double outline of a heart in red ink, done right between her breasts. From that heart, and on both sides, flowers in blue and foliage in green extend from it, travel under each of her breasts, circling them, and climb upward towards her small but thick nipples. It is a piece of simplistic design—hearts, leaves, flowers, a symbol of renewal, of life—and I am disappointed, I expected something more dramatic, edgier, darker, but even her tattoo was nice and friendly.

Her breasts, almost within reach of my touch, are enticing.

Lisa quickly covers her breasts and lowers her top.

15.

I was too exhausted to do anything last night, which made it easier to promise to wait one more day. We were now even. I tricked her into showing me her breasts. I didn't care for that naive tattoo but I liked her small, firm breasts, and her thick nipples that I imagined quite sensitive to the touch. She had a nice body, despite her round head. It's not about that. I actually wanted to see how far she would take this helpfulness. I don't even like her that way and she has a partner who she loves. I had no right to play such stupid games. Embarrassed, she had ran out of the house. It will keep her away, which is good, but nevertheless it was mean of me.

I get her tattoo, it was as much about love and nature as it was about a belief that love had the power to give birth to something new, something beautiful, natural and innocent, maybe children. And of course, the breasts as the canvas in her case was not something sexual but maternal. If that was it, she had it bad, but it's her problem.

I glance at my alarm clock and realize that it is already noon. I slept for so long, too long, but I was exhausted, emotionally drained. I did wake up a few times, tossed around a bit, but fell asleep right away. Even the itchiness inside the cast seems to have subsided. I count the hours in my head—thirteen hours of sleep, I can't remember the last time I slept so long and so deeply. I pick up my phone and turn it on. I have four messages. I don't want to hear what they have to say, although I can guess. Last night, before going to bed, I emailed my letter of resignation to my school principal and to the Board of Education's HR department. It was such a great relief to know that I didn't have to go back. They would be calling about that, about me emptying my desk or something. I'll deal with them in due time. It's all paperwork from this point on. There is no hurry; the school would have dealt with the supply teacher. I also fished out from the recycling bin one of those realtors' glossy and oversized calling cards and put it on the dining room table, to be looked at later.

I am more and more comfortable with only using my right hand, it's beginning to feel natural. The cast helps.

I pull off the covers, sit up and light a cigarette. I let my mind wander and let myself enjoy the smoke. Interestingly and surprisingly, I get a bit aroused when I replay in my mind how she lifted her bra. It is obvious she won't come again. It is too bad, I could have used her help but not the way she wanted to help me. I can handle it on my own, I have to. I have read enough and I have everything I need.

In my pyjamas, cigarette smoked and stubbed, I go and get the chainsaw and try to figure out the best way to try it on the bones. I get them out of the fridge and take one out of the packaging. The problem is going to be how to anchor the bone so that it does not move while I cut it. I will have the same problem with the arm and need to find a solution that will work for both.

The saw looks like a small toy. I leave it on the dining room table and go into the basement to get the long, all-usage, orange extension cord and plug it in. I will need to minimize the mess, maybe cover everything with sheets.

If I had a table saw or that round saw that one can bring down with a lever, it would be so much easier.

I will need to keep the arm or the bone steady while I cut into it, and I need to make sure that the cut is straight, so that it can heal better.

In the basement I find what I need, that same roll of grey duct tape that I had already used on the filing cabinet, and pieces of two-by-fours left over from an unfinished job my mother had started many years ago. They are all approximately the same length, about three feet, and they will do the trick. It takes me a couple of trips with my one arm, but I bring everything I need to the kitchen and lay it on the small table.

Sitting down, I use my knees as vise grips with the roll of duct tape firmly jammed in between them. I use my right hand to pull up a strip. I stick the start of that strip to the edge of the table, which frees my right hand to grab the scissors and to cut a good length from the roll. In that manner I cut eight pieces, long enough to go around the bone shank and the two-by-four a number of times.

I place the bone in the middle of the two-by-four, and sit on it, so that it won't move, letting part of it stick out. I press one end of the tape to the side of the two-by-four, making sure it holds and then wrap the tape tightly over both the wood and the bone; the strip is long enough to go over five or six times. I get up, turn the plank around and repeat the process for the other side.

With a black marker I draw a thick line as to where I want to do the cutting—I want to see how straight I can cut through the bone with one hand.

Unfortunately, as soon as I am done, I also realize that the whole thing moves when I push the bone around. The duct tape works for the bone but I need to do something else with the two-by-four, to strap it onto something in order to prevent it from budging.

I try different but ineffective ways to tape the wood to something in the kitchen, near the sink.

If I put the piece of lumber on the floor, I can stand on it with one foot on each end, and bending down, cut where the line is. I try the position and although awkward it works, since the wood won't move. It will be good to test the saw that way, but that position won't work for the arm. I have to find a better method.

I hear footsteps on the porch.

I stop what I am doing and listen.

There is a knock on the door.

I put the two-by-four on the counter, and holding the saw in my right hand, I go to the front.

Lisa is standing there. I knew it would be her. Part of me still hopes that she might understand. Part of me still hopes that she might help, but on my terms. She has on a light, pink summer dress that suits her thin body. Her hair is tied back, which makes her face appear rounder than it really is, she looks like a pink lollipop. It is a sexy, low-cut dress and she is not wearing a bra. She knows my weakness, but it won't work.

"What are you doing here?"

She ignores my question and walks right in.

"Lisa, *what are you doing here*, you shouldn't be here."

I need to get rid of her and quickly.

"I came to watch, sign your cast, whatever, I hope you don't mind?"

"I do mind, you can't, please get out." I have had enough.

I stand in front of her, blocking her from coming any further. I put my hand on her shoulder and slightly push her back.

She doesn't move.

I lift the chainsaw over my head for dramatic effect and point it at her.

She doesn't move.

I step on the extension cord that's on the floor, to hold it down, and plug in the saw.

She doesn't move.

I lift up the saw, wave it in the air and am about to press the trigger, to show her that I mean it, that I am ready to cut something, to scare her.

"Stop!" she screams.

16.

I stop, and release the trigger as she yells, "You are doing it all wrong, moron, you are going to kill yourself." And although I don't trust her, I hear her out—butchering myself is not what I want to do.

"What do you know about chainsaws, Lisa?"

"Plenty, I grew up on a farm. You already forgot. I told you, you are not a good listener."

I don't believe her, she is thinking of some other way to delay me. It won't work, not even if she bares her breasts again.

"I am serious, at least I can show you how to hold it. Not because I want you to do it, I can just see the terrible mess you will make. Did you secure the handguard and the chain?"

She comes towards me and takes the chainsaw from my hands and puts it on the kitchen counter. I keep my eyes on her.

"It has to be pushed up and locked in to protect your hand." She presses down on a lever and pulls up the protective gear until it locks into place. I watch her jiggling breasts as she bends to adjust the chain.

"Here… oh, wait. Also you should know, you have to gently press down, but not too hard when you start. Let the teeth slowly grind into the wood… careful with the kick-back as there will be some resistance when you first start, it can push you off and with one hand you'll be more susceptible. You have to hold tight when that happens."

She moves around as she shows me how she would cut an imaginary log. How to position one's body. I don't know what to make of this. What she says makes sense and I am grateful for the information. She is still trying to help me. She positions herself at an angle, facing me, and smiling. She looks her old self. Maybe she finally understood.

"Lisa, why are—"

She doesn't let me finish, pirouettes, quickly unplugs the saw from the extension cord and runs out of the house with it.

I should have seen it coming. What does she think that I am going to do, let her get away with it?

I go to her house.

I try the door, and of course it is locked. I knock, and there is no answer. I go to the back of the house, tap on a window, also no answer. I know that she is there. I can see her through the light drapes. She pulls the blinds down. I return to the front and with my closed right fist bang loudly and rattle the glass of the screen door.

"Lisa, open the fucking door and give me back my saw or I'll keep yelling until the neighbours come out." I knock some more.

"I'll make a scene. The neighbours will come out, explain *that* to Thomas."

I hear a muffled "no," a "go away," and a "stop this madness," from somewhere in the middle of the house.

"You know I am just going to go and buy another one if you don't open the door."

I hear footsteps as she comes closer to the door and she says distinctly, "I'll call the cops on you."

"And say what?"

She opens the front door but leaves the screen door locked.

She looks at me and gives me that compassionate, incredulous, serious stare that says, "I feel sorry for you."

"Jack, what will it take to stop you?"

I know that she means well, but this has nothing to do with her. It is not about being a good neighbour or even a good friend, it is about me and only me.

"Nothing!"

"Jack, talk to me."

She hasn't understood my problem.

"Listen, Lisa, and this is the last time I will defend myself to you. It's like conversion therapy. Most professionals and even the public have abandoned the idea that conversion therapy works. By making me live with my left arm, you and society in general are forcing me into daily conversion therapy."

"It's not the same, Jack."

"Really?"

I turn away and start walking back to my house. I had remembered something.

"Keep the saw," I yell.

I hated mother's proverbs that passed for discussions but now that she is no longer here, they surface whenever they feel like it.

"There are many ways of killing a pig other than by choking it with butter," was one of her favourites.

Once inside, I go back to thinking about the issue of the moving two-by-four, and how to best anchor it. The wood needs to be secured, tied down, or glued to something.

I have nothing in the bedroom, in the kitchen or the dining room that I can use to strap it down, or... I have the answer.

I grab the two-by-four with the taped bone shank and carry it around while I look. I won't use the table since it might wobble but the kitchen counter is perfect. It's just Formica on top of wood and that will do just fine.

I don't need the chainsaw either.

The kitchen will always be my mother's domain. It's synonymous with her. She spent a lot of time cooking for the lodgers and for me in here, she planned her meals from the early morning, made sure she had what she needed and prepared what the lodgers said were delicious meals. Unfortunately, with so much time spent preparing the dinners, she had little time to deal with me. I remember that to get her attention, I would run into the kitchen and pretend that I got hurt while playing.

A hammer and some long nails are all I need. It's a simple solution. I easily find that in the basement where all the tools are neatly hanging on the wall, and all the nails of different lengths have their own tin—my mother was meticulous to a fault.

Back at the kitchen counter, I try my new idea, but it doesn't work. I can't hold the nail and hammer at the same time with one hand. I try propping up the nail with kitchen utensils to no avail.

The chainsaw was another stupid idea, like the experiment.

Using only one arm is silly at this stage, I could wiggle my fingers sticking out of the cast and use them to anchor the nail, but it's important to me not to use the left hand for anything, and I want to keep it that way. I know that there is a solution to this—I just need to find it.

The nail keeps falling down. I push it into the wood with my hand to make it stand up so that I can begin to hammer it, but it's not deep enough, the nail slips and falls to the floor as I let go. After a few more failed attempts, I have another thought.

From the workbench in the basement, I pick up the small drill that my mother would use to make all kind of repairs around the house. Mother knew how to use these tools better than me. I must have been a total annoyance to her. Unwilling or incapable of doing the most minor work around the house. Although I recall that every time I tried, I was told I was doing it wrong.

As a kid, I would pace up and down the kitchen, purposefully get in her way, and make small hurt noises until she noticed. I then made up stories about falling and hurting my arm, my leg, sometimes pretending to cry. It was only then that she would stop what she was doing and look after me, and say a few kind words before shooing me away.

Holding the drill between my thighs, I open and slide a small bit into the widening mouth, and then tighten it with the key that is kept attached to the cord. I plug it into the orange extension cord and drill a small hole in the two-by-four. I stop just a couple of inches from the end. I do the same to the other end of the wood.

I place the two-by-four, with the duct-taped bone strapped to it, horizontally along the counter. I put the first nail in one of the holes, where it fits snugly, and hammer away. Not something that I am good at, especially with one hand and with nothing holding the wood, but at least the nail is standing up and it more or less works.

Of course, the attention from my mother would not last. I always wanted more. Never knew if it was me wanting too much or her not giving enough.

I miss more often than not, hitting wood, bone, counter and nail. I should stop thinking about my mother and concentrate. She would be turning in her grave if she knew what I was using her kitchen for. She always worried about me eating right, never asked a penny from my wages, although I made sure to deposit a quarter of what I earned into her account. After a while, as I hit the nail with more consistency, I feel it go through the counter and I continue hammering until the nail is completely in. I'll need to remove them later with a crowbar.

I do the same to the other nail. I am a little bit better with the second one. One last hard bang and the job is done.

The wood is now solidly attached to the counter. I try to budge the bone. Nothing, solid as a rock, the duct tape is still doing the trick. The two-by-four does not shift either when I attempt to dislodge it.

A cigarette is my reward. I want a drink badly but I want to be completely sober when I do this. I content myself with walking around the kitchen, taking deep drags of the cigarette and letting the ashes fall on the ground.

My attempt to be deliberately messy does not last long—I get on my knees and wipe the ashes off the floor.

I put the pipe-cutting hacksaw and the crowbar that I had brought up from the basement on the counter. I tighten the two wing nuts that hold the thin but powerful blade of the hacksaw. I put some olive oil on a paper towel and apply it to the blade, something I had seen my mother do. The sharp teeth shred the paper towel as I go along it.

With the saw in my right hand, and cigarette dangling, I start cutting, and at first the blade slips to either side of the marked line. I try again, slowly, and apply downward force with each stroke. I repeat the motion until a small groove begins to appear along the black line. Neither the wood nor the bone shifts. I quickly note that slow, long strides work best, and that this saw, used to cutting steel and copper, has no issue with bone. I lean my body into it, the left arm in its cast dangling uselessly to my side. It does not take long, I hear a crack as the bone is cut right through and the saw reaches the two-by-four.

I admire the perfect cut along the black mark. At least I now know that it can be done and that it's not too difficult, and that it does not take very long.

I am glad Lisa played that last little game, the hacksaw is much better than any chainsaw. The idea of switching to a handsaw came to me while she stubbornly refused to give me back the electric one. In effect, everything that she has done to anger and to delay me has forced me into a better understanding of what I have needed to do, to better solutions. I suppose I should be grateful

I go downstairs to the laundry area and bring back small, clean towels. Lots of them.

I use the crowbar to dislodge the wood from the counter.

I stub the cigarette out.

I take the rubberized strings that I had difficulty finding at the Rexall pharmacy, lay one of them straight on the counter, position my left arm on top of it, and with my right hand make a loose knot. It takes a couple of tries, since the elasticized string keeps undoing itself. Eventually the knot stays together and using my teeth to hold one end, I tighten it as hard as I can with my right hand. I tie the other one about four inches below and in the same way so as to create two very taut tourniquets.

The duct tape is still on the counter. I find the beginning of the roll, hold it between my thighs, pull out a strip, tape it to the edge of the counter and cut a long band, about the size of those I had cut earlier. I repeat the process and get eight of them.

Of course, it was understandable that mother was always busy. It was hard work running the house and being a single mother to an unwanted child, but understanding it did not make it any better. I had difficulties sorting out where she could have been a better mother and where I could have been a better son. Things are a bit clearer now.

I grab one of the two-by-fours with the pre-drilled holes and lay it on the kitchen counter. I position my left arm on it, push the wood over the edge of the counter, grab one of the pieces of the duct tape and roll it around the plank and around the left wrist that is in the cast several times. Holding tight, I straighten the left arm along the two-by-four, and I duct-tape above the line I know too well. I am thankful that the cast is only to the elbow. I do it again with another strip along the wrist and one along the upper muscle. I use all the pre-cut pieces of tape. I make sure that everything is very tight, that the arm is immobile and that the wood comes along whenever I move the arm. The tourniquet digs into me exposing the bulging veins on each side.

I place the now duct-taped arm length-wise, on an angle facing the wall. That seems to work best as it allows both holes, the one in front of my fingers and the one half-way between the elbow and my armpit, to be on the counter and easily reached for nailing.

I make sure that the rags are nearby, that the hacksaw is within reach, and that the crowbar is also accessible.

I put the nail into the first pre-drilled hole and hammer. It is easy to manage and when I do miss, I hit the side of the two-by-four and not my hand. The nail easily digs into the counter and holds the wood in place. I do the same with the second nail by slipping it into the hole closest to me, and because of the proximity, I find it easier to hammer. Very quickly, I have the two-by-four, and me, firmly secured to the counter.

I grab the hacksaw by its handle.

The blade touches my arm and I quickly recoil and tense up. The blade feels oily and cold against the skin. And for the first time this week I'm scared, really scared.

I put the handle of a wooden spoon in my mouth and bite down.

I take another deep breath and gingerly begin to slice through the first layer of skin, expecting the worst and it *is* the worst. My left hand instinctively tightens into a half-fist, nails grinding into the cast. A stabbing pain accompanies the saw as it punctures the skin, while blood pours out of a thin cut. I pull the saw away.

I can't do this, I don't have the nerve. *I am sorry*. No. Yes.

Three short successive breaths and I cross-cut deeper along the width of the arm—more blood comes rushing out, squirting over the arm, over the wood, on the counter, running to the floor. The pain is sharp and incessant, and there is no turning back. I breathe loudly, hiss and grind my teeth but it does little to reduce the searing agony.

It hurts too much, I stop again, remove the saw from the cut, and push the rags against that first cut. I hold everything tight. The blood flow slows down.

It is my last chance to stop, to go back to the way I was, to forget all of this. No.

I pick up the saw again, and find the same spot. I move the bloodied rag out of the way and with more determination than I have ever mustered, I cut through an artery, and now there is more blood and more of that sharp, relentless pain. I fear that I am going to faint.

I resist and grab more rags to absorb the blood, to put around the blade and the cut.

I have to keep going. I can't stop. I can feel the bone under the blade. The pain is unbearable—I grit my teeth as much as I can, suck my breath, tighten my fist, while I try to no avail to cut through the bone. Every attempt sends agonizing shivers through my back. I bite hard on the wooden spoon.

"Feckin'… bloody, feckin' hell… "

I add more force to the saw, and my scream comes out as a long, muffled grunt. I heave uncontrollably, unable to ignore the excruciating pain. Leaning my whole body into it, I saw furiously, the thin blade bending with each back and forth. The sharp teeth of the hacksaw grind through the outer layer of the bone and quickly create a groove, I press down harder as I saw faster and faster.

I can't breathe. Choking, I spit out the spoon. Gasping and heaving to catch my breath, I continue cutting.

The pain is now slightly more bearable as the saw cuts right through the bone. The pain has hit a plateau, still there, but endurable. I am not going to die. I am not going to faint. I am just numb.

Finally, the bone cracks and the sharp pains start again as the saw shears the outer skin, and hits the two-by-four.

17.

I am trembling as I run. The tourniquet has not worked as I thought it would. There is more blood than I thought there would be. I am pressing as hard as I can with my right hand against the stump, but the blood does not stop. I am hemorrhaging.

I get next door and with my right elbow, bang on the glass, my foot also kicking the door.

She opens, and her face turns white.

"What—"

"Please…"

She doesn't need to speak and so she doesn't.

Lisa takes over pressing hard on the wound as she guides me to her kitchen. It's my first time in her house and it feels strange, in so many ways, to be here. Both of us are pressing on the wound as we are walking. She tightens the upper tourniquet and wraps a towel around the stump which she also ties very tightly, numbing the arm but slowing the flow of blood.

She puts my right hand against it, indicating that I should press. I do and feel no shame or guilt at touching that part of the arm that has always belonged to me.

"Lisa, I wasn't going to bother you, I do have a small emergency kit at home, the blood… I got scared. I don't want to die."

Lisa looks at me, eyes wide open, incredulous.

"Please don't call 911, please," I beg her.

She doesn't answer, walks away for a moment and comes back with a small bag which she puts on the table. She takes out what looks like the white plastic emergency kit I had bought a couple of days ago, but this one is labeled "suture kit."

Lisa takes out a pair of blue medical gloves, opens the cupboard, takes down a deep dish, fills the bottom with rubbing alcohol and puts in it the instruments she takes out of her kit. I feel disoriented, the pain immobilizes me and I am glad that she is here, that she knows what she is doing. I have no way to respond to anything. I feel overwhelmingly numb, as if this is not happening to me. She sits me down, and I am so grateful for her help.

She takes the instruments out of the dish and puts them on a tray that she has also disinfected.

Lisa is not talking, she takes over, doing what she needs to do, in full nursing mode, and I let her.

She pulls me up and takes me over to the sink. Removes the towel that is already soaking in blood and is starting to stick to the opening, turns the faucet on, wets a clean cloth and washes away as much of the blood as possible from the rest of the stump. The pain comes back.

When clean, she pours liquid on pieces of cotton and as she swabs my cut, I scream in pain and pull away.

She grabs the stump with her gloved hands, drags me back and inspects the cut. She swabs some more and although it is sheer agony I don't dare say anything. I let her nurse me.

Blood is no longer gushing, and she picks up a small scalpel from the paper towel.

"What are you doing?"

She starts cutting away small pieces of flesh that are sticking out.

"Lisa, it hurts, stop it."

She doesn't, holds my arm tight, and I have to trust her. She uses a scissor-like instrument that was also on the tray, picks up the suture needle with it and begins patching me up. She pushes the needle straight down into the flesh, pierces through to the other flap of skin and then pulls up. Straight down and straight back up. I watch her hands. She doesn't hesitate.

It doesn't hurt too much, not after the earlier pain, more like multiple needle shots. It does not take her long to sew the skin over the bone.

When finished, she slowly removes the tourniquet, washes the edges again, puts some cream on the wound, bandages it and gently inserts the stump into a medicated cloth sleeve.

She hands me the chainsaw.

"Go see a doctor tomorrow, you have lost a lot of blood… and never speak to me again."

18.

I can't get a handle on what exactly I am feeling, there are too many converging and contradictory thoughts, good and bad in equal parts, but mostly I feel very tired, lethargic, and disoriented. It has been a week since I solved the problem that has haunted me ever since I can remember. The severed arm, a repository of all that was toxic in my life, is now in a box, under the sink, still wrapped in bloody rags. I have cleaned up as much as I could. I have put away all the tools. Everything is back to *normal*. The only reminder of what I did are the four holes on the white Formica counter.

I have a need to constantly look at my left side to make sure the arm is not there. I touch the medicinal sleeve and feel the rounded stump inside. It still hurts when I touch the stitched wound; a sharp pain shoots right through my shoulders. I have not left the house for the past week, and I have not seen a doctor as Lisa had ordered. I have all I need to keep the stump healthy and free from infection. I keep the shades down. When needed, I order from the numerous takeout menus I have accumulated, but the reality is that I have had very little appetite. I only eat the food that my Internet connections indicate will help me regain some of my blood loss.

I doubt I will ever cook in this kitchen.

I am getting better at my morning routines. It is much easier without the arm, I don't have to pretend or be tempted. I fight disorientation. The battles against the arm were so much a part of me and now that the fighting is done, I am left with an emptiness or lack of purpose. It's not a bad thing; I am calmer. I don't feel the need to smoke as much anymore.

What I am certain of is that it was the right decision.

Lisa has not tried to contact me and that is also good, I am not ready to talk to people, even her. I will be forever thankful for her help, and that, one day, I will tell her.

It was, after all, simply about getting rid of what was toxic and keeping what was healthy.

Although, one thing that I know is that Lisa and the others were wrong. In the past week, it had become so evident. The arguments about this being psychological or hard-wired are a moot point; that was the wrong battle, the wrong argument. The fact is that notwithstanding the pain, and there is a lot of it, and the traumatic act itself, I feel at peace with what I did. I believed that the arm was not mine, and as such it wasn't, period. That is what people don't understand, I am not sure I can explain it either, but in the end, it does not really matter. I am better off without the toxicity that handicapped me most of my life.

Once in a while, I go to grab my left arm, accompanied each time with the dread that it is still there since it feels like it is still attached, but all I grasp is air and I am filled with a sense of relief.

Taking care of my stump takes up most of my days. I read about how best to take care of it on the Internet, and watch for any sign of infection. I am glad that I had purchased all that I needed and in such abundance.

I do things in small doses. I read a bit, watch TV, but that being a wasteland, I rely more and more on the radio. I listen to music. I sleep a lot during the day, since the healing and the pain keeps me awake at night, but even that is different from when I couldn't sleep, from when my mind kept racing, revving up my anxieties and fears to keep me awake.

Today I feel stronger, buoyed by the news that my union will deal with my formal resignation from teaching. I told them that I had had an accident and couldn't attend to the paperwork. They were very understanding, would take care of it for me, and wished me well.

After breakfast, I go down to the basement and bring up the bags filled with my mother's old clothes, the bags that I had unceremoniously thrown down there. I line them up in the hallway.

Under the sink, I retrieve the ball of soiled rags that has the arm, still in its cast, and add longer, clean towels around it until I can't see any more dried blood. I drag in one of the bags from the hall, open it, remove half of my mother's old dresses and sweaters, put the newly wrapped arm in the bag, and shove back what I had taken out. I tie it and place it where the others are.

Today is also garbage day.

I look outside to make sure there is no one around, and take the bags, one by one, to the curb. I go to the side of the house and grab the large garbage bin and with my right hand, guide it to the sidewalk. There, I open it and throw in two of the garbage bags, including the one containing the arm. I leave the others beside it.

As I turn to go back, Lisa, pushing her own garbage bin, comes out from between the houses. She is in tights and an oversized sweater. Our eyes meet.

"Hi, Lisa."

She does not answer.

"Thank you for all you did. For what you did for me. You saved my life."

She still does not answer, but stops walking and looks at me. Peers at my left side, at the dangling, empty shirt sleeve. She looks paler than usual, not wearing any makeup, almost like the first time we met, but the cheerfulness is gone.

"I am sorry..." I start again, but she doesn't seem interested, she shakes her head and walks away.

I am truly sorry that she is disappointed in me, but it was not her place to try to "save" me from myself, I wasn't her story. For too long, I had allowed others to write my story. I had lived in other people's shadows, as my mother had before me, and I am only sorry that mom had not had the chance to escape it.

I walk towards the house and look at it. The home I have lived in my whole life, both a sanctuary and a prison.

Selling the house and moving away, like getting rid of the arm, is also the right thing to do. I feel sorry for Lisa, she has her own issues to deal with, and I am sorry that I can't help her, but there are decisions that one needs to make on one's own terms, there is only so much one can understand about someone else. I will leave her my email address and I'll listen if she ever wants to talk. I will check in on her, write to her, and maybe with time, with whatever she decides, we can become friends, real friends.

Inside the house, I pull up the blinds, let the sun in, look to my left side, nod and smile.

I think that I will start by taking a trip, and do something that I have always wanted to do: go to Europe, probably Ireland, and maybe stop in Paris, see the Rodin Museum.

Other Recent Quattro Fiction